CINDERS

A MODERN CINDERELLA LESBIAN ROMANCE

CARA MALONE

Copyright © 2018 by Cara Malone

All rights reserved.

No part of this book may be reproduced in any form or by any electronic or mechanical means, including information storage and retrieval systems, without written permission from the author, except for the use of brief quotations in a book review.

ACKNOWLEDGMENTS

As always, thank you to Claire Jarrett, my editor, for challenging me and making me a better storyteller.

Thank you to Mayhem Cover Designs for the phenomenal book cover.

And thank you to my readers, many of whom have also become friends. My gratitude is eternal.

CINDERELLA

BY JACOB AND WILHELM GRIMM

A rich man's wife became sick, and when she felt that her end was drawing near, she called her only daughter to her bedside and said, "Dear child, remain pious and good, and then our dear God will always protect you, and I will look down on you from heaven and be near you." With this she closed her eyes and died.

The girl went out to her mother's grave every day and wept, and she remained pious and good. When winter came the snow spread a white cloth over the grave, and when the spring sun had removed it again, the man took himself another wife.

This wife brought two daughters into the house with her. They were beautiful, with fair faces, but evil and dark hearts. Times soon grew very bad for the poor stepchild.

"Why should that stupid goose sit in the parlor with us?" they said. "If she wants to eat bread, then she will have to earn it. Out with this kitchen maid!"

They took her beautiful clothes away from her, dressed her in an old gray smock, and gave her wooden shoes. "Just look at the proud princess! How decked out she is!" they shouted and laughed as they led her into the kitchen.

There she had to do hard work from morning until evening, get up before daybreak, carry water, make the fires, cook, and wash. Besides this, the sisters did everything imaginable to hurt her. They made fun of her, scattered peas and lentils into the ashes for her, so that she had to sit and pick them out again. In the evening when she had worked herself weary, there was no bed for her. Instead she had to sleep by the hearth in the ashes. And because she always looked dusty and dirty, they called her Cinderella.

One day it happened that the father was going to the fair, and he asked his two stepdaughters what he should bring back for them.

"Beautiful dresses," said the one.

"Pearls and jewels," said the other.

"And you, Cinderella," he said, "what do you want?"

"Father, break off for me the first twig that brushes against your hat on your way home."

So he bought beautiful dresses, pearls, and jewels for his two stepdaughters. On his way home, as he was riding through a green thicket, a hazel twig brushed against him and knocked off his hat. Then he broke off the twig and took it with him. Arriving home, he gave his stepdaughters the things that they had asked for, and he gave Cinderella the twig from the hazel bush.

Cinderella thanked him, went to her mother's grave, and planted the branch on it, and she wept so much that her tears fell upon it and watered it. It grew and became a beautiful tree.

Cinderella went to this tree three times every day, and beneath it she wept and prayed. A white bird came to the tree every time, and whenever she expressed a wish, the bird would throw down to her what she had wished for.

Now it happened that the king proclaimed a festival that was to last three days. All the beautiful young girls in the land were invited, so that his son could select a bride for himself. When the two stepsisters heard that they too had been invited, they were in high spirits.

They called Cinderella, saying, "Comb our hair for us. Brush our shoes and fasten our buckles. We are going to the festival at the king's castle."

Cinderella obeyed, but wept, because she too would have liked to go to the dance with them. She begged her stepmother to allow her to go.

"You, Cinderella?" she said. "You, all covered with dust and dirt, and you want to go to the festival?. You have neither clothes nor shoes, and yet you want to dance!"

However, because Cinderella kept asking, the stepmother finally said, "I have scattered a bowl of lentils into the ashes for you. If you can pick them out again in two hours, then you may go with us."

The girl went through the back door into the garden, and called out, "You tame pigeons, you turtledoves, and all you birds beneath the sky, come and help me to gather:

The good ones go into the pot,

The bad ones go into your crop."

Two white pigeons came in through the kitchen window, and then the turtledoves, and finally all the birds beneath the sky came whirring and swarming in, and lit around the ashes. The pigeons nodded their heads and began to pick, pick, pick, pick. And the others also began to pick, pick, pick, pick. They gathered all the good grains into the bowl. Hardly one hour had passed before they were finished, and they all flew out again.

The girl took the bowl to her stepmother, and was happy, thinking that now she would be allowed to go to the festival with them.

But the stepmother said, "No, Cinderella, you have no clothes, and you don't know how to dance. Everyone would only laugh at you."

Cinderella began to cry, and then the stepmother said, "You may go if you are able to pick two bowls of lentils out of the ashes for me in one hour," thinking to herself, "She will never be able to do that."

The girl went through the back door into the garden, and called out, "You tame pigeons, you turtledoves, and all you birds beneath the sky, come and help me to gather:

The good ones go into the pot,

The bad ones go into your crop."

Two white pigeons came in through the kitchen window, and then the turtledoves, and finally all the birds beneath the sky came whirring and swarming in, and lit around the ashes. The pigeons nodded their heads and began to pick, pick, pick, pick. And the others also began to pick, pick, pick, pick. They gathered all the good grains into the bowls. Before a half hour had passed they were finished, and they all flew out again.

The girl took the bowls to her stepmother, and was happy, thinking that now she would be allowed to go to the festival with them.

But the stepmother said, "It's no use. You are not coming with us, for you have no clothes, and you don't know how to dance. We would be ashamed of you." With this she turned her back on Cinderella, and hurried away with her two proud daughters.

Now that no one else was at home, Cinderella went to her mother's grave beneath the hazel tree, and cried out:

Shake and quiver, little tree,
 Throw gold and silver down to me.

Then the bird threw a gold and silver dress down to her, and slippers embroidered with silk and silver. She quickly put on the dress and went to the festival.

Her stepsisters and her stepmother did not recognize her. They thought she must be a foreign princess, for she looked so beautiful in the golden dress. They never once thought it was Cinderella, for they thought that she was sitting at home in the dirt, looking for lentils in the ashes.

The prince approached her, took her by the hand,

and danced with her. Furthermore, he would dance with no one else. He never let go of her hand, and whenever anyone else came and asked her to dance, he would say, "She is my dance partner."

She danced until evening, and then she wanted to go home. But the prince said, "I will go along and escort you," for he wanted to see to whom the beautiful girl belonged. However, she eluded him and jumped into the pigeon coop. The prince waited until her father came, and then he told him that the unknown girl had jumped into the pigeon coop.

The old man thought, "Could it be Cinderella?"

He had them bring him an ax and a pick so that he could break the pigeon coop apart, but no one was inside. When they got home Cinderella was lying in the ashes, dressed in her dirty clothes. A dim little oil-lamp was burning in the fireplace. Cinderella had quickly jumped down from the back of the pigeon coop and had run to the hazel tree. There she had taken off her beautiful clothes and laid them on the grave, and the bird had taken them away again. Then, dressed in her gray smock, she had returned to the ashes in the kitchen.

The next day when the festival began anew, and her parents and her stepsisters had gone again, Cinderella went to the hazel tree and said:

Shake and quiver, little tree,
    Throw gold and silver down to me.

Then the bird threw down an even more magnificent

dress than on the preceding day. When Cinderella appeared at the festival in this dress, everyone was astonished at her beauty. The prince had waited until she came, then immediately took her by the hand, and danced only with her. When others came and asked her to dance with them, he said, "She is my dance partner."

When evening came she wanted to leave, and the prince followed her, wanting to see into which house she went. But she ran away from him and into the garden behind the house. A beautiful tall tree stood there, on which hung the most magnificent pears. She climbed as nimbly as a squirrel into the branches, and the prince did not know where she had gone. He waited until her father came, then said to him, "The unknown girl has eluded me, and I believe she has climbed up the pear tree.

The father thought, "Could it be Cinderella?" He had an ax brought to him and cut down the tree, but no one was in it. When they came to the kitchen, Cinderella was lying there in the ashes as usual, for she had jumped down from the other side of the tree, had taken the beautiful dress back to the bird in the hazel tree, and had put on her gray smock.

On the third day, when her parents and sisters had gone away, Cinderella went again to her mother's grave and said to the tree:

> Shake and quiver, little tree,
>   Throw gold and silver down to me.

This time the bird threw down to her a dress that was

more splendid and magnificent than any she had yet had, and the slippers were of pure gold. When she arrived at the festival in this dress, everyone was so astonished that they did not know what to say. The prince danced only with her, and whenever anyone else asked her to dance, he would say, "She is my dance partner."

When evening came Cinderella wanted to leave, and the prince tried to escort her, but she ran away from him so quickly that he could not follow her. The prince, however, had set a trap. He had had the entire stairway smeared with pitch. When she ran down the stairs, her left slipper stuck in the pitch. The prince picked it up. It was small and dainty, and of pure gold.

The next morning, he went with it to the man, and said to him, "No one shall be my wife except for the one whose foot fits this golden shoe."

The two sisters were happy to hear this, for they had pretty feet. With her mother standing by, the older one took the shoe into her bedroom to try it on. She could not get her big toe into it, for the shoe was too small for her. Then her mother gave her a knife and said, "Cut off your toe. When you are queen you will no longer have to go on foot."

The girl cut off her toe, forced her foot into the shoe, swallowed the pain, and went out to the prince. He took her on his horse as his bride and rode away with her. However, they had to ride past the grave, and there, on the hazel tree, sat the two pigeons, crying out:

Rook di goo, rook di goo!

There's blood in the shoe.
The shoe is too tight,
This bride is not right!

Then he looked at her foot and saw how the blood was running from it. He turned his horse around and took the false bride home again, saying that she was not the right one, and that the other sister should try on the shoe. She went into her bedroom, and got her toes into the shoe all right, but her heel was too large.

Then her mother gave her a knife, and said, "Cut a piece off your heel. When you are queen you will no longer have to go on foot."

The girl cut a piece off her heel, forced her foot into the shoe, swallowed the pain, and went out to the prince. He took her on his horse as his bride and rode away with her. When they passed the hazel tree, the two pigeons were sitting in it, and they cried out:

Rook di goo, rook di goo!
There's blood in the shoe.
The shoe is too tight,
This bride is not right!

He looked down at her foot and saw how the blood was running out of her shoe, and how it had stained her white stocking all red. Then he turned his horse around and took the false bride home again.

"'This is not the right one, either," he said. "Don't you have another daughter?"

"No," said the man. "There is only a deformed little Cinderella from my first wife, but she cannot possibly be the bride."

The prince told him to send her to him, but the mother answered, "Oh, no, she is much too dirty. She cannot be seen."

But the prince insisted on it, and they had to call Cinderella. She first washed her hands and face clean, and then went and bowed down before the prince, who gave her the golden shoe. She sat down on a stool, pulled her foot out of the heavy wooden shoe, and put it into the slipper, and it fitted her perfectly.

When she stood up the prince looked into her face, and he recognized the beautiful girl who had danced with him. He cried out, "She is my true bride."

The stepmother and the two sisters were horrified and turned pale with anger. The prince, however, took Cinderella onto his horse and rode away with her. As they passed by the hazel tree, the two white pigeons cried out:

> Rook di goo, rook di goo!
>   No blood's in the shoe.
>   The shoe's not too tight,
>   This bride is right!

After they had cried this out, they both flew down and lit on Cinderella's shoulders, one on the right, the other on the left, and remained sitting there.

When the wedding with the prince was to be held,

the two false sisters came, wanting to gain favor with Cinderella and to share her good fortune. When the bridal couple walked into the church, the older sister walked on their right side and the younger on their left side, and the pigeons pecked out one eye from each of them. Afterwards, as they came out of the church, the older one was on the left side, and the younger one on the right side, and then the pigeons pecked out the other eye from each of them. And thus, for their wickedness and falsehood, they were punished with blindness as long as they lived.

ONE
FIRST BLOOD

The painting was one of those abstract deals.

He'd been standing in front of it for the last thirty minutes and he'd be damned if he could make anything out of it. There were colorful paint splatters and a few geometric shapes. For a minute or two, he thought he saw a duck in the bottom right corner, but it was just a bunch of nonsense shapes. Pieces of paper cut and pasted randomly onto the canvas, then splattered with more gobs of meaningless paint.

The longer he stared at it, the more certain it seemed that the artist was mocking him and his fruitless search for the hidden message within the painting.

Sure, let me waste half an hour of my day looking at this fucking thing, *he thought,* trying to figure out what you're saying to me. Really, it's just a great big middle finger pointed directly at me.

The tiny foam board plaque hanging on the wall at the bottom right corner of the canvas seemed to prove his *suspicions. It had the artist's name and the title of the piece printed on it.*

Anthony Rosen. "Two Lovers at Dusk," 2018. Enamel on canvas.

Yeah, as if that clears things up, *he smirked, looking again for anything even remotely resembling a pair of lovers... or anything humanoid at all.* Lovers, my ass.

There was nothing there. It was all inside the charmed mind of Anthony Rosen, and yet here he was, with his so-called artwork hanging in the Grimm Falls Museum of Art. Anyone could make something as unintentional as this. It was a Jackson Pollock with a few extra scraps of paper glued on for good measure.

Hell, *he thought*, even I could do something this terrible.

What made Anthony Rosen so special?

He put his hands in the pockets of his jacket and his fingers found a small cylinder in his right pocket. He slid his thumb along the plastic casing until he found the metal wheel at the top of the lighter. The metal was slick and warm beneath his touch, and even though he'd only just picked it up this morning, he'd already gotten into the habit of rubbing it like a worry stone.

Well, back *into the habit.*

He hadn't bought a pack of smokes in three years because everyone knew they were killers.

Not great for job hunting, either – a lot of companies won't even look at you twice if you show up to your interview smelling like an ashtray. All they see is insurance money going up like so much smoke.

But this morning was different. When he walked up to the counter at the gas station where he stopped for a cup of coffee every day, he pointed to the Winston Lights on the rack behind the clerk. "The gold pack," he'd told her, and just like that, it was as if he'd never quit. Of course, he needed to buy a lighter to go with the cigarettes, so he snatched one from the Bic display and slid it across the counter to her.

He was tearing the cellophane off the cigarette pack before he was even out of the gas station. He was so itchy for a smoke, he left his coffee cup on the counter and didn't figure out his mistake for another twenty minutes. But that first, long inhale never tasted better, even if it did make him cough and hack a bit.

And then he'd come to look at "Two Lovers at Dusk" – really look at it, because up until today, he hadn't been able to see a thing. Now that he was here, the lighter wheel was begging to be flicked.

He looked around, but there weren't many people in the museum at this hour. It was the middle of a weekday and besides the group of third graders who had marched obediently and disinterestedly through the Grimm Falls Local Artists exhibit twenty minutes ago, he was alone.

He had to admit it was satisfying to see how little those kids cared about Anthony Rosen and his featured artwork. When they showed up, he stepped aside and watched them. Did a nine-year-old give any more fucks about abstract expressionism than he did?

Turns out, no.

They walked past the paintings in the exhibit room in

an orderly line that had been orchestrated by a teacher who seemed determined to get this over with. Some of them glanced at "Two Lovers at Dusk," and some didn't even bother.

He had a crazy urge to hold out his hand for a high-five from those kids. They knew ego and favoritism when they saw it. Then the kids were gone, moved on to another exhibit hall, and it was just him and the painting again.

And the lighter.

He hadn't seen so much as a docent in the last five minutes – it was all too perfect. Like the universe wanted him to show Anthony Rosen where he really stood.

He took out the lighter and flicked the wheel once, not hard enough to ignite the flame but enough to let off a thrilling spark. It felt good, like scratching an itch. Same as that first cigarette this morning.

The four he'd smoked since then didn't taste quite as good as the first, but that was to be expected. How much could you really ask of a pack of smokes?

The itch came back stronger this time. All he wanted was a little taste – a tiny bit of relief. It felt good to buy that pack of Winstons on impulse this morning, and where had he ever gotten by ignoring his impulses, playing by the rules?

Nowhere fast.

He flicked the lighter again, letting the flame catch this time. His heart was pounding and he could feel every nerve ending in his body spring to life, on high alert.

He reached forward and touched the flame to the bottom corner of the canvas, right next to Anthony Rosen's foam board plaque. He just wanted to singe it, to leave his mark. If a disaster like this got a little bit blackened, nobody would even notice, right?

The flame licked across the bottom of the canvas and he blew on it, but it didn't go out. The fire really loved the enamel paint and it kept spreading across the front of the painting.

He could have blown harder, or used the sleeve of his jacket to smother the flame. Hell, there was a fire extinguisher mounted to the wall not more than twenty paces away. But as he watched the orange fire bubbling up the paint and eating Anthony Rosen's smugness, he felt calm. The way the fire danced along the bottom of the canvas frame was almost elegant.

He watched for a minute, entranced, and when smoke began to curl up toward the sprinkler system, he stuffed the lighter back into his pocket and walked away. He ducked into a nearby exhibit on pointillism and a few seconds later, a docent shuffled briskly up the hall.

"Fire!" she yelled, her voice cracking with panic.

Then the museum director ran up the hall, his fingers twisted into his thinning hair as he told the docent, "Call the fire department!"

He heard the sound of the fire extinguisher being yanked off the wall, and the whoosh *of chemicals as it obliterated the flames and what was left of the painting. Inside the pointillism exhibit, he slid his hand back into his pocket, stroking the lighter wheel once more. An unexpected smile formed on his lips. Today was a great day to pick up smoking again.*

TWO
CYN

Cynthia Robinson arrived at the museum in style – hanging off the side of a fire truck with sirens blaring. It was how she would choose to travel anywhere, if she had her way, because the sound of the sirens and the weight of her uniform always got her adrenaline pumping.

As it turned out, it was a tad much for the situation at hand.

There was a class of third graders lined up in the parking lot, most of them with their noses in their phones and paying no attention at all to the screaming red fire engine as it pulled up to the curb. There were also a handful of volunteer docents, a security guard – who happened to be Cyn's stepbrother – and the museum director, a tightly wound man named Orson.

There was no smoke or flames to be seen, and the museum itself was quiet. Normally when the fire department got called, it was because the alarms inside the building in question had gone off, and they were usually still blaring when Cyn and her crew arrived. The only thing that was blaring today was Orson.

"I just don't understand how anyone could do such an awful thing!" he exclaimed as Cyn hopped off the truck and went to meet him. "It's simply unpatriotic!"

"Why don't you show us what happened?" Cyn asked, trying to sound calm and reassuring to balance out his frenetic energy. "Has the fire been contained?"

"Yes, I put it out myself," Orson said, puffing out his chest with pride. "I'm good in a crisis."

Who told you that lie? Cyn wondered. The way his whole body was practically twitching with distress gave her second-hand anxiety. She nodded to her stepbrother, who was standing with the docents, looking bored and scratching the scraggly hair on his chin. "Come with us, Drew. You might be able to help."

He gave her a look that made it clear he was unenthusiastically obeying her order. They were never the loving type of step-siblings, and she knew taking orders from her got under his skin. That's why she was determined to be gentle and deferential when she asked him what he knew about the fire.

Cyn, Orson and Drew went inside the building, along with a couple of guys from her crew. The others stayed outside with the truck, winning over the kids by letting them play on it while they waited to find out if they would be needed.

It was strange to be alone inside the museum. It wasn't too long ago when Cyn herself was one of those third graders here on a field trip, and now it was her job to keep it safe.

Orson led the group down a few winding hallways until they got to the Local Artists exhibit, then he hung his head as he presented the charred remains of a canvas at the end of the hall. It was unrecognizable – a blackened and drippy mess of browns and grays where all the paint had either burned or melted into a homogenous goop.

Orson was right about one thing – an attack on the artwork of a Grimm Falls native felt like a personal attack on Cyn's own soul. Part of the reason she became a firefighter was to protect this town she'd come to love like it was a part of her.

"I blame myself," Orson said while Cyn pointed her guys to the canvas, instructing them to make sure the danger was past. "Although I don't know how I could possibly have predicted this. Who would be motivated to do something like this? I nearly vomited when I heard one of my docents yelling 'fire'."

"Did you see anything, Drew?" Cyn asked.

"No," he said. "I was keeping an eye on that group of elementary kids, making sure they kept their fingers off the art, you know?"

Cyn nodded, committing his response to memory, as well as everything else she saw and heard. Paintings didn't just spontaneously combust, so she'd have to write up a report for the fire investigator after they were done here. She'd been a firefighter for four years now, and she learned pretty early on that the smallest details sometimes make the biggest difference.

Like the way Orson was practically choking back sobs while he watched Cyn's crew inspect the canvas. Overacting? Maybe, but she'd seen a wide variety of stress reactions in the last few years and an abnormally large reaction to a relatively small event wasn't out of the ordinary. Especially considering how much the museum meant to Orson.

"Hey, Anthony Rosen," one of Cyn's guys – Gleeson – said as he read the name off a small, slightly blackened plaque on the wall. He turned and shot a mischievous grin at her as he asked, "Wasn't that your old high school flame?"

Cyn felt her cheeks coloring. She'd gotten used to the way the guys at the firehouse ribbed each other – and her – nearly constantly, but her history with Anthony wasn't a subject she liked to dredge up.

She was just trying to pick out the perfect snarky response when she heard someone behind her say, "Nice choice of words, asshole."

She turned to see her best friend, Gus, sauntering up the hall in his policeman's blues. *Thank you,* she thought, telepathically sending the message to him. Not that she needed rescuing, but there was nothing like a little police-firefighter rivalry to deflect attention from herself.

"I was just teasing old Cinders about her straight phase," Gleeson said, holding up his hands defensively. Then he grinned and said, "Anyway, I was thinking about motive. How did that relationship end, again?"

Cyn rolled her eyes heavily and said, "I caught him under the bleachers with another girl on prom night."

He quirked an eyebrow at her and said, "Sounds like revenge to me."

"A dish best served five years later?" Cyn asked.

Anthony certainly hadn't been in the running for any *World's Best Boyfriend* awards back then – that was for sure – but Cyn hadn't exactly given him a chance. Ever since she moved here, she'd only had eyes for the blue-eyed, blonde-haired, hopelessly out-of-reach Marigold Grimm. Anthony was nothing more than an attempt to appease her stepmother, and Cyn had been hurt when she found him kissing someone else under the bleachers, but the hurt didn't last long.

Certainly not five years after high school ended.

"He's a jerk," Drew said. "Probably had it coming from any number of people he's pissed off."

"Dude, I saw him get into a bar fight last weekend," Gleeson said. "Forgot about it until just now. I wasn't close enough to hear what it was about, but anybody mad enough to take a swing at a guy at the bottom of the ninth with two strikes is worth talking to."

"Good," Gus said, pulling out his notepad and flipping to a fresh page. "Do you know who it was?"

"Braden Fox. He's kind of a hot head, too. Definitely not the first bar fight he's ever been in."

That was one of the best things about Grimm Falls, in Cyn's eyes. It was a deceptively big city that felt a lot like a small town. Most everyone who stuck around long enough knew each other, and that was great if you wanted to feel safe leaving your door unlocked, or feel like a part of a genuine community.

Not so great if you wanted to go around getting in bar fights and setting paintings on fire without getting noticed.

"Thanks, I'll check him out," Gus said. Then he nodded at the charred canvas and said, "And we have to get the fire investigator in here. That was no accident."

THREE
MARIGOLD

Marigold Grimm was practically flying around the estate.

"Slow down, girlie," her assistant, Emily, teased as Mari came rushing down the grand staircase with a clipboard in her hand. "You're acting like this is the biggest event we've ever hosted."

"It is," Mari said. "To me, anyway."

Her father's retirement party was still seventy-two hours away and Emily was right to give her that *calm down, crazy woman* look. Mari had been up and down these stairs at least half a dozen times before breakfast and she knew she was driving Emily and the rest of the staff crazy with her demands to check and re-check everything.

Are the caterers aware of our gluten-free guests?

Will the tulips still be at peak bloom if they're delivered the day before the event?

Has the gravel in the parking lot been raked?

Those were the questions that had been racing through her mind all week, each one accounted for on her clipboard. It all had to come together perfectly, and if that meant being a thorn in the sides of everyone working in Grimm House until the party on Saturday night, Mari was willing to make the sacrifice.

She was also, apparently, willing to sacrifice breakfast, sleep, and good arch support. Her feet ached from days of running around the fifty-thousand-square-foot manor and the sprawling estate beyond. Even though the party would take place on a fraction of that space, she knew how guests liked to wander and she was determined that everything should be perfect.

Most importantly, she needed her father to find everything *just right*.

"What about the fifty-three weddings we did last year?" Emily reminded her. "Plus, we have the annual service awards ceremony, the Christmas gala... all the kids love the Easter egg hunt on the lawn, there's the volunteer work you do at the teen center, oh, and the summer concert series is a big hit-"

"I get it," Mari said, pausing at the bottom of the stairs and shifting her weight to her toes to give her aching heels a rest. "We do a lot of events. They all go well. We have a great staff here. Thanks for the reminder, Em."

"It doesn't sound to me like you're planning to calm down at all," Emily said. "Trust me, we have this under control."

"I do trust you," Mari said, and it was true even if

Emily could see the *but* coming a mile away. "But I have a lot riding on this event. I can't afford to calm down."

This was the first event that her father had handed over to her completely. She'd made a rock-solid argument that it wouldn't be appropriate for him to plan his own retirement party, and when he agreed, Mari took over the planning with great enthusiasm.

"You know your father's going to hand the estate over to you, right?" Emily said, giving her a pitying look. "You don't even have siblings to compete with."

Mari smiled. Emily thought she was being ridiculous – they'd had that conversation *many* times since her father mentioned retirement last Christmas. "I'm not worried about getting the estate. I'm worried about having to share it."

"Spoken like an only child," Emily said with a laugh.

"Do you know if the linens have arrived yet?" Mari asked.

She was looking at her clipboard, and the expanse of white space beside *linens* on her list. Almost everything else had at least one tidy little checkmark next to it, but those linens were becoming troublesome. She couldn't stand in the entryway all morning talking about birth order theory. She rocked back on her heels to give her toes a break.

"Yes," Emily said, sounding exhausted by the subject. "They're being ironed in the laundry room as we speak. They'll be everything you could possibly want from table linens, perfectly crisp and lime green."

"Lime green?!"

Emily let out a snorting laugh that echoed in the tall-ceilinged entryway. "They're white. Your face though-"

"Jerk," Mari said. She put a neat checkmark next to *linens*, making a mental note to check on the ironing herself in a little while. Then she said, mostly to herself, "I should check on the garden next, make sure it's been properly weeded..."

"The landscaper came yesterday afternoon," Emily said. "He said it's the best flower garden we've had since your mother tended it herself."

Mari had to pause to revel in that. "Really?"

"Yeah," Emily said.

Mari smiled, then said, "Well, I'm going to take a look at the chocolate cosmos. They were looking a little wilty during the dry spell last month, but I think they're coming back. Do me a favor?"

"Not until you tell me what it is," Emily said.

"Let me know if you see Ryan," she said. "I sent him into the city to confirm some details with the caterer, but I imagine he'll be back soon."

"Can't you confirm catering details over the phone?" Emily asked. Mari gave her a wink and Emily shook her head. "You sly dog, you. Poor guy probably doesn't know the meaning of the term *fool's errand*."

Mari felt a twinge of guilt. Ryan was the estate's marketing director and the third in command, after Marigold herself. If her father had his way, she and Ryan would run the estate together after he retired, and if Mari had *her* way, Ryan would be updating his resume the day after the retirement party.

With a glowing recommendation from her, of course. She wasn't a monster – she just didn't want a partner, and especially not Ryan. She answered Emily with, "When my father is congratulating me on an event well-executed, I want to be able to tell him it was all me."

"So when I see Ryan, I'll send him your way so you can give him more meaningless busywork," Emily said. "Got it."

"Thank you," Mari said.

"You're welcome," Emily said. Mari headed for the service hallway that would take her out to the garden. Behind her, Emily called, "And put on some sneakers! Those flats are ridiculous."

"They're Coach," Mari objected over her shoulder.

She went outside, her blue eyes narrowing in the brilliant, late morning sun. The expansive estate stretched out before her – a view that Marigold never tired of. Grimm House sat on forty acres of lush grass, sparkling ponds, and secluded woods. There was a stone amphitheater built into the hillside about two acres from the house, where the thespians and musicians of Grimm Falls performed regularly, and a large wooden pergola beneath which Mari had watched dozens of happy couples wed.

The property had belonged to her family ever since the founding of Grimm Falls itself, when Marigold's great-grandfather, Rudolph Grimm, traveled there from Germany. He had the estate built to honor his father, the celebrated author Wilhelm Grimm, and he'd brought many manuscripts and hand-written drafts to fill the house's library.

That rich history was something Emily understood academically, but not emotionally. It only made Ryan see dollar signs, but Marigold and her father both felt the tradition of the property in their blood.

Mari turned to the left as she walked out the door, heading up the wide stone path that would take her to her favorite part of the estate – the garden. There was greenery spilling over the path, climbing arches and hanging overhead. All of it had the effect of making Marigold feel like she was walking into a fairy tale every time she entered the garden, and it never failed to take her breath away for just a moment.

The garden covered more than an acre of land. It grew every year with new plants and interesting features, like the circular meditation labyrinth that Mari had built after a college trip to India, and the koi pond that her father told her had always been on her mother's wish list. The garden had been her mother's pride and joy and she'd nursed it just like a baby through her childless twenties and thirties. Marigold had been their miracle baby, conceived long after the doctors had given up on Philip and Anita Grimm's chances.

Mari knew every flower and every plant by name by the time she was ten. She never let the landscaper work in the garden without her. She had the koi pond installed on her twenty-fifth birthday - the twenty-fifth anniversary of her mother's death - and she sat by it often.

Just like Mari could feel the history of Grimm House in her blood, she could feel her mother's presence in the cool dirt beneath her hands, or the sweet perfume of delicate rose buds, or the peaceful song of robins in the morning. She could think of no better place to honor her father's career, although this morning, the garden could hardly be called peaceful.

There were staff members all over, carrying long wooden tables and setting them up in a long row on the central path from which the garden branched out. Despite Emily's assurances, the setup appeared to be going slower than Mari would have liked.

In three days' time, all the influential people in Grimm Falls would be here in their finest tuxedos and gowns, expecting a gourmet meal. None of the chairs were set up yet, and the string lights that would hang over the tables and illuminate the meal were still laying in neatly coiled heaps on the side of the path.

Mari blew a ringlet of light blonde hair out of her face, clutched her clipboard to her chest, and got to work. By the night of the party, there would not be so much as a burned-out bulb over the table, a wilted mum in the centerpiece, or a leaf out of place in her garden.

FOUR
CYN

Cyn finished writing up her report on the museum fire the day after the incident and because things were quiet at the firehouse, she decided to walk the five blocks to the police station to deliver it.

She'd taken extra care in writing down her impressions of the scene, and ran through each of her five senses in her mind while she tried to pick out any details that could be helpful to the fire investigator. She hadn't picked up on anything that she thought was significant – and neither had anyone else on her crew – but the fire wasn't sitting right with her, and you never knew what might be a clue to the investigator's trained eye.

In her four years as a Grimm Falls firefighter, Cyn had worked on only five arson cases. One was the work of bored teenagers who underestimated the power of fire, and the other four cases had never been solved.

That wasn't out of the ordinary. Accelerants like gasoline or lighter fluid, or even strategically stacked newspapers, could easily go unnoticed in the rush to secure the area and put out the fire, and arsonists don't exactly walk around proclaiming the success of their crimes. People burn things to hide secrets, or as seemed to be the case with Anthony Rosen's painting, to seek revenge. That was why it was so important for Cyn and her crew to be observant when arriving on the scene of every fire.

What color is the smoke?

Where's its origin?

Are there any bystanders who seem suspicious?

Firebugs like to admire their work, and often, they like to hang around to watch the first responders fight the blaze. There were just a bunch of museum employees and kids at the scene this time, and Cyn couldn't see evidence of an accelerant in use. But the more she racked her brain for details, the more she wondered about those four unsolved cases. Did they have anything to do with this one?

It was unlikely. Arsonists weren't the type to lay low – they set a single fire to accomplish their goal, or in the case of serial offenders, they tended to work in a short timeframe. Still, Cyn wanted to mention the cases to Detective Holt when she turned in her report. Even with the pathetically low conviction rate for arson – or maybe because of it – Cyn knew he would leave no stone unturned. He was good at his job just like she was good at hers, and they both wanted the same thing – to protect Grimm Falls.

Of course, the best scenario would be securing an

easy confession from Braden Fox, the guy who'd gotten in a bar fight with Anthony. Nothing tied a case up in a neat little bow like a simple act of revenge.

Enjoying the way the afternoon sun baked down on her skin, Cyn took her time walking to the police station. She took the stone steps two at a time to get her heart pumping, then stepped aside and held the station door open for an elderly woman with silver hair and a walker who was on her way out.

"Thank you, dear," she said as the wheel of her walker got stuck on the door jamb. Cyn lifted it out, a little swell of pride in her chest at being of use to the woman.

Then while she waited for her to clear the door, a sparkle of green caught Cyn's eye. She looked down to street level, where an emerald green BMW was pulling into a parking spot on the curb across the road.

Cyn's heart skipped a beat.

It was silly. The sight of that car alone was powerful enough to make her heart seize whenever she saw it around the city. Fortunately, or unfortunately, it didn't happen too often, but when it did, the car was almost always parked in front of Green Thumb Nursery's downtown storefront.

Cyn waited, and a moment later she was rewarded with a rare glimpse of the driver. Marigold Grimm stepped out of the car, her blonde hair flowing in the breeze. She flipped it over her shoulder, wavy and perfectly styled like she'd just stepped out of a shampoo commercial. She was wearing a pair of khaki shorts that rode high up the long stems of her legs. On her feet were a pair of loafers that probably cost more than Cyn's entire wardrobe, and the neckline of her loose-fitting blouse drew Cyn's attention.

She'd never seen Marigold with so much as a hair out of place. Cyn often wondered if she was the type of girl who got up two hours early just to get ready for the day. It was that, or little birds flew into her window every morning to help her get dressed.

Cyn didn't have a hard time imagining either possibility, and either way, it was working for her. Marigold was Grimm Falls royalty, and she looked the part.

"I said thank you," the old woman said sharply.

"Hmm?"

"You can let go of the door now, sweetie," she said, and Cyn realized that the woman and her walker were a good three feet away, at the top of the accessibility ramp. "I appreciate the dedication, though."

Cyn's cheeks colored slightly and she nodded at the woman, wondering sheepishly if she'd noticed the direction of her gaze. When she looked back across the street, Marigold was just slipping through the Green Thumb door.

Probably getting ready for her father's high-profile retirement party.

It wasn't the first time Cyn had lost track of reality when Marigold Grimm was around, and it probably wouldn't be the last. Cyn had been hypnotized by her since the first time she'd laid eyes on her, when she was twelve and Marigold was fifteen – three years too old to bother with her. Marigold was Drew's age and he'd had just as fierce a crush on her as Cyn had. Cyn took a small amount of consolation in the fact that Marigold never seemed to give him the time of day, either.

Cyn turned to go inside the police station and found Gus with his arms folded across his chest, grinning at her. She rolled her eyes. "What?"

"Nobody told me we hired a door greeter," he said. "Firehouse not paying you enough so you have to moonlight for us?"

"*Somebody's* got to have the courtesy to hold doors for the elderly," Cyn said. "Unless you'd rather let the paramedics get involved after someone wipes out on these impractical stone steps."

Gus looked over Cyn's shoulder, then said with a grin, "Or maybe it has something to do with a certain green BMW across the street."

"Maybe," Cyn confessed. Gus was her oldest friend and she knew the futility of trying to hide her crush from him – it had been well-documented over the years, and Gus knew it all. Not that there was much to tell – Cyn had spoken to Marigold about three times in her life, and somehow that was enough to keep the flame burning.

Marigold Grimm simply could not be forgotten.

"Why don't you grow a pair and finally ask her out?" Gus asked.

"She doesn't know I exist," Cyn said. "Not to mention the fact that we probably don't even play for the same team."

"I know," Gus said. "But don't you think it would be

so much easier to get over her if you actually *heard* her reject you? It's time to grow out of that crush, Cinders."

"You're right," she said, although she couldn't fathom wanting anyone else. "Is Detective Holt around? I have to turn in my report on the museum fire."

"Yeah, he's at his desk," Gus said. "I'm on my way out to lunch. You wanna grab a burger with me when you're done?"

"Sure," Cyn agreed. She stepped into the building and let the door swing shut, nearly clipping Gus's foot with it to pay him back for the smart remarks.

FIVE
PRACTICE MAKES PERFECT

It was two in the morning and he couldn't sleep because of that itchy feeling. It had been growing ever since he watched that canvas burn, and tonight it got him out of bed.

He wound up at the old red barn on County Route 10 without much thought. It was like his feet led him there of their own accord, and when he stood in front of the building, his thumb rolling over the wheel of his lighter, he knew it was right.

About three miles outside of town, no witnesses as far as he could see – the house that went with the barn had been razed in the nineties to make room for more lanes on the highway. Traffic in and out of Grimm Falls was much heavier now than when he was a kid, but the barn was well back from the road, and anyway, there weren't many people driving at this hour who would care about him and his lighter.

He pulled it out of his pocket and gave the wheel a

flick. The little orange flame was comforting, like a friend or at least an ally.

The barn, on the other hand... well, there would be no love lost when he burned it to the ground. It was at least a century old, its wood siding rotted and hanging tentatively from rusty nails. There were more holes than patches of solid wall, and its red paint was dirty and flaking off all over the ground.

Probably lead-based to boot, *he thought.*

He was here to satisfy the peculiar new itch he'd acquired, but he took pride in the knowledge that he was also doing Grimm Falls a favor. This barn was where generations of the city's teenagers gathered to drink their parents' booze, and it was a total death trap.

He'd fix that tonight, with one strike of his lighter wheel.

He poked his head inside first. There was no sign of recent debauchery when he arrived, but he was just here to light a little fire – he didn't want to hurt anyone. Looking inside the barn – carefully, lest the old, dry-rotted support beams give way in a preemptive act of God – he remembered his own youthful indiscretions. Nothing too bad – just a little partying on prom night.

He hadn't thought of the barn in years, but it was starting to come back to him now. Prom night had been okay. It would have been better if he'd gotten invited to the real after party, but back then he knew how to make his own fun.

Yeah, he was going to enjoy making his own fun again tonight.

He used the flashlight on his phone to gather up some dry grass and packed it around the base of the building. If he'd been thinking and not just walking, he would have brought something like gasoline, or lighter fluid, to get the job done quicker. But if the barn burned slowly, he'd have longer to enjoy it.

He lit as many small fires as he could in the dry brush, then he walked into the tall grass surrounding the building. All that land used to be cornfields, tall and green, providing a perfect illusion of solitude. Now it was just weeds.

The barn burned delightfully slowly.

The flames ate their way up the plank siding, crackling and popping as the fire consumed the old wood. By the time he heard the first support beam crash to the ground inside, the fire was burning bright as day and he could feel the heat on his cheeks. He knew it was time to go when he heard the fire engine in the distance, its siren blaring. But he couldn't move. Instead, he crouched low in the overgrown weeds and watched as half a dozen of Grimm Falls' finest hopped out of the truck and aimed their hoses at his creation.

SIX
CYN

Cyn put her hand to the necklace that was weighing her down, like an anchor yearning for the sea floor. Objectively, she could appreciate its beauty – a strand of large, glossy turquoise beads that hung together like raindrops gathering on a gold chain.

Subjectively, they were totally not her style.

The necklace came from her stepmother's boutique – the one in New York with all the newest arrivals. Samantha had given it to Cyn for her birthday one year, and even though Cyn had never enthusiastically worn a piece of jewelry in her life, she made a point to choose something from her over-stuffed jewelry box whenever her stepmother was around. There was no pretending at this point that Cyn would magically transform into *Cynthia*, the feminine, heterosexual, jewelry-loving and fashionable stepdaughter Samantha always wanted, but wearing the jewelry did seem to make family dinners go a little more smoothly.

Tonight they were eating at the Enchanted Inn, one of Cyn's favorite places, and the ostentatious necklace made her feel self-conscious as she walked into the restaurant. The turquoise would have looked beautiful on a more feminine woman's delicate collarbones – Marigold's, perhaps, the color of the stones offsetting her light blue eyes. Draped over the fully-buttoned collar of Cyn's neatly starched gray button-up, it was out of place.

She was out of place.

"Cynthia." She turned to the sound of her name and saw Samantha's bejeweled hand snapping impatiently in the air.

Cyn joined her family at the back of the restaurant. Samantha was in a stylish dress more suited to the streets of New York than the quaint Enchanted Inn. Cyn's father, Elliot, sat at his wife's side in a tweed jacket he almost definitely didn't choose for himself. And Drew looked bored with his elbow on the table and his fingers combing through the hair on his chin.

"Sorry I'm late," Cyn said, sliding into the empty chair across from her stepmother. "There was a fire last night that's looking like another arson attack and I had to run my report over to the police station before I came."

"Another?" Samantha asked. "What was the first?"

"The one at the museum last week," Drew said. "Remember? Somebody torched Cyn's old boyfriend's painting."

"Oh right, Anthony," Samantha said as the waiter came around to take Cyn's drink order. She smiled. "He was a nice boy. Tell me again why you didn't hang onto him?"

"He cheated on me on prom night," Cyn said. *Among other reasons.* She turned to the waiter and asked for a glass of lemon water. Samantha and her father were sharing a bottle of pinot and Drew was kicking back a bottle of beer, but Cyn had never been much of a drinker. She'd tried it in high school, as most people do, but it hadn't gone well.

The lemon water would keep her hands busy while she waited for the main course, and more importantly if Samantha was going to make a beeline for her troubled dating history, it would also keep her mouth busy.

"Apparently, the arson attack was over a football bet or something," Drew said to his mother as the waiter walked away. "The guy, Braden Fox, got into a bar fight with Anthony the weekend before the fire. What an idiot."

"Actually," Cyn said, unable to keep herself from correcting him, "Detective Holt talked to Braden and he had a solid alibi. He was at work on the other side of town when the fire broke out, and his boss vouched for him, so now we're back to square one. We're not even sure if the barn fire is related to the museum fire, or if we've got two separate arsonists on our hands."

"Is that better or worse?" her father asked.

"I'm not sure," Cyn said. "If they're isolated incidents, then separate is probably better. There was no evidence of accelerants at either scene, so it's possible that the barn fire was an accident - just kids being kids."

That idea comforted her. The fire itself was most definitely intentionally set – that barn had stood alone on County Route 10 for the last hundred years, and the burn patterns on what was left of the structure by the time Cyn and her crew extinguished the fire told them there were multiple points of origin. The best-case scenario was a couple of rowdy teenagers and a dare that had gone too far.

The worst case was that this was the beginning of a serial arson case.

"Alright, well that's enough talk about crime at the dinner table," Samantha said, downing the remains of her wine glass and then pouring another. "I have some news. My New York boutique is going to have a feature in Nylon magazine this winter."

Elliot beamed at her, lifting his glass to salute the good news. Samantha clinked her wine glass against Drew's beer bottle, and then Cyn's lemon water.

"Congratulations," Cyn said. "That's amazing. What's the feature about?"

"They're going to focus on the family aspect of the business, how I built my national brand up from one little shop in Grimm Falls," Samantha said, beaming with pride as she took another sip of wine. Cyn prepared for what she figured must be coming – an invitation to New York to play up the family optics, along with a swift reminder that she wasn't who Samantha expected her to be for the cameras. Instead, her stepmother said, "So that means I'll be spending a lot more time in New York, making sure the shop is in tip-top shape for the photoshoot."

"Is Dad going with you?" Cyn asked.

"No, I'm sure I'd just be underfoot," her father said with a small chuckle. "I'm going to be holding down the fort here."

Cyn smiled. She lived in a small carriage house above the garage of her father and Samantha's home, but she didn't come over to the main house very often. With Samantha out of town, this could be a good excuse for Cyn and her dad to spend some time together. "Maybe we can cook dinner one of these nights. My buddy at the firehouse, James, just took a cooking class with his wife and he's really been getting into it. I'm sure he'd give me a good recipe to try."

"No need," Samantha said curtly. "I arranged for a personal chef to cook for Elliot while I'm gone."

Her father said nothing, just took another sip of his wine and looked away from Cyn.

"Oh, okay," Cyn said. Then she turned to Drew to keep the conversation going without betraying her disappointment. "How's the security work going?"

Drew had gotten that job about six months after Cyn began working at the fire department, and he'd never quite gotten over the self-imposed stigma of being a security guard, as opposed to the badge-wearing, gun-toting, authority-wielding cop he really wanted to be. He shot her a withering look and said, "It's fine. They have me working a little overtime at Grimm House for some big event tomorrow night."

"Oh yeah," Cyn said. "Philip Grimm is retiring. My chief's going to that party – the most influential people in the city will be in attendance."

"And Drew," Samantha said with a little snort as she took another sip of wine.

"I bet it'll be fun," Cyn said. "You'll probably get a meal out of it, and just spending the evening in that huge, beautiful estate is a dream. I can't wait for the service awards ceremony this year."

"First step, getting a seat at the table. Next step, win an award of your own?" her father asked. "There's a Firefighter of the Year award, isn't there?"

"Yeah," Cyn said. "But it's pretty selective – you have to do something big to earn it, and there's a lot of seniority and politics that goes into it…"

She trailed off in the middle of her list of reasons why the award would never go to her. She couldn't deny having dreamed about it, mostly on sleepless nights when she was on call at the firehouse and nothing much was going on. But the idea of getting all that attention was both exciting and horrifying, especially when she knew that Marigold Grimm would be watching.

"You're right," Samantha said. "That sort of thing takes connections, and you've never been very good at that. Now, for my Nylon feature, I had to talk to people all up and down the garment district."

Cyn took another sip and found the bottom of her water glass. She'd never been very good at getting Samantha's attention, or at least not the good kind of attention. She hadn't wanted to work in the boutique when she was a kid, nor did she have any interest in looking the part. The day she came home and declared she was going to be a firefighter, Samantha began calling her only by her full name.

Cynthia.

So prim. So proper. So *not* her.

"You know, I get a plus one for the awards ceremony," Cyn said. "It's a black tie event and two hundred of Grimm Falls' most influential people will be there. Would you like to go with me, Samantha? I bet you could drum up some more publicity for your boutique."

"No publicity is bad publicity," Samantha said. "Yes, it will be a nice opportunity to rub elbows with the mayor, and the Grimm family. I've been wanting to set up a pop-up boutique in that enormous foyer for years."

Cyn glanced at her father, feeling guilty for not inviting him, but she really only had one extra ticket. Besides, if Cyn offered it to him and Samantha wanted it instead, there's no way he would have denied her.

SEVEN
ATTACK NUMBER TWO

His next target was the first one to be deliberately chosen.

The painting had been more or less an accident, but the barn was a real thrill. The crackle as the flames bit into the wood, the curls of smoke rising into the night and disappearing into the dark sky, and the smell of a good char, like a barbeque...

Just like last time, he waited until the early hours of the morning to make his move. Unlike last time, he brought something to speed the fire along. He parked his car at the road and lugged two five-gallon gas cans all the way up the long driveway of Grimm House at three in the morning. His arms were aching by the time he arrived in the garden behind the estate.

It was all set up for the elder Grimm's retirement party. There were fancy wooden tables set up all in a row down the center aisle of the garden, about a hundred chairs on either side. String upon string of lights were *hung overhead, although he could only see the outline of their shapes – luckily, they were unlit and he moved freely in the dark.*

He was wearing black from head to toe - the red gas cans were the only colorful thing that might reflect the light of the fire, but he wasn't planning to stick around like he had at the barn. That fire had simply been for practice, but this one had a message.

It was about pride and elitism, and about the false sense of community that everyone in Grimm Falls worked so hard at constructing, only to cast people aside when their usefulness ran out. And it was about Marigold Grimm, who seemed perfectly aware of the bewitching power she held over people, and just didn't care.

In just sixteen hours, two hundred of Grimm Falls' most celebrated residents would be parading up that extra-long gravel driveway and stepping out of their luxury vehicles in their finest clothes. They'd be expecting caviar and classical music, but he was going to give them another type of spectacle all together.

This was going to be fun.

He set the gas cans down on the end of the long table and looked toward the house. Well, mansion would be a better word for it. The building was ostentatiously large, sprawling on and on, farther than he could see in the dark. There were a few lights on in the front of the estate – probably lights that were never turned off – but he could see no sign of movement inside.

Most importantly, there weren't any lights visible on the third floor, where he knew the live-in staff's bedrooms were located, as well as the living quarters of Marigold Grimm herself. He'd seen it once, on a field trip in middle school to learn about local history. It was strange because Marigold was in his class, touring her own estate and doing most of the lecturing. Maybe it was even stranger for her, but she'd held her head high and kept her expression robotic and poised as ever.

He wondered then if she considered herself to be on the same level as the rest of their classmates. She was always aloof, and she'd only gotten more unapproachable with age.

We'll see if this rattles her at all, *he thought, his hand going instinctively to the lighter that now lived permanently in his front jacket pocket, beside a half-smoked pack of Winstons. It probably wouldn't take the fire department long to respond, but he hoped there would be an opportunity to see her reaction.*

A quick Google search had told him she still lived at the estate, although her father had purchased a penthouse apartment downtown about five years ago, when the urge for contemporary architecture and convenience had become too great. At least, that's what he'd told a reporter for the Grimm Falls Gazette.

It was incredible what one could find on the internet these days, like a list of the most effective fire-starting chemicals, or instructions for a Molotov cocktail that sounded really convenient about now. A couple of those would have beat the hell out of carrying ten gallons of gas all this way.

He popped the cap off one of the cans and the pungent

odor of gasoline wafted into the air. It cloyed in his throat, momentarily preventing him from taking a breath. It wasn't pleasant like the more organic smell of the barn fire – just a little brush, some old, dry wood, and his trusty lighter.

But aside from the long row of tables, the Grimm House garden was full of greenery. Live plants wouldn't burn so easy, and he wasn't interested in merely torching the furniture. He wanted to see Marigold's precious garden burn.

He wanted to see her watch it burn, the thing she always seemed to care more about than anyone else. That would be something to behold.

He started with the tables just because they'd catch the fastest. He used up the contents of an entire red can walking down the long aisle, sprinkling gas on the tables and chairs and then coming back up the other side. Then he grabbed the second can and started dousing all the plants in the area. The garden was enormous – it would be impossible to burn it all, but he'd certainly try.

While he walked, enjoying the gravel under his feet and the sound of gasoline splashing like raindrops on broad leaves, the itchy feeling started coming back to him again. It was his new favorite sensation and he couldn't wait to satisfy the craving again.

When the second can was almost empty, he made a little gasoline trail for himself, then threw the can down and took out the lighter. He pulled a cigarette out of his pack and tucked it between his lips, then flicked the lighter wheel. He sucked the little orange flame into the tip of his cigarette, letting the first plume of smoke rise into the air. Soon to be joined by a whole lot more.

Then without letting the lighter go out, he reached down and touched the flame to the gas-soaked gravel.

It caught fire in an alarming WHOOSH, the flame much bigger and more immediate than he was expecting. He felt the heat on his face and jumped back, his heart climbing into his throat as he patted his clothes and stubbed his toes in the gravel.

"Shit," he hissed.

He'd singed the toes of his favorite work boots and his cigarette had dropped from his mouth and into the flame. That was okay – it would burn up as the fire had its way with the garden – but he couldn't wear those boots around town anymore without rousing suspicion.

Once he determined that he definitely wasn't on fire, he watched the gas finish tracing its path to the tables and into the flowerbeds. It might stink and it was definitely heavy as all hell, but gasoline was certainly effective. The whole area was engulfed in a matter of seconds, the green plants letting off plumes of smoke as they curled in on themselves.

There was something beautiful about the way the flames danced with each other.

He stood still for a minute, entranced with his creation, and then a window on the third floor of Grimm House flew open and someone shouted, "Who's there? What the hell are you doing to my garden?"

Time to go.

EIGHT
MARIGOLD

Mari was awake long after everyone else in the house had gone to bed. That wasn't unusual for her, and it was pretty much inevitable on the eve of her very first solo event.

The Grimm House staff was incredible – especially Emily, who did everything Mari asked of her and even found it in her heart not to tease her too mercilessly over how anal retentive she was being about the details. The tables and chairs were all set up, the linens were ironed and ready to be laid out in the afternoon, and the house had been cleaned from top to bottom – all fifty-thousand square feet.

Emily had even appeased Mari when she wanted to test out half a dozen different table settings, then test them all out one more time to make sure she'd chosen the best, classiest option. (In the end, they went with gold chargers, delicate ceramic plates, and a single white mum tucked into each cloth napkin because they were her mother's favorite flowers.)

The bar was stocked, the string quartet was confirmed, and Mari had been able to keep Ryan busy with the catering details all day yesterday. Her clipboard was positively filled with neat little pencil marks, and all that was left to do was one final check in the afternoon to make sure it was all coming together as planned.

She should have been sleeping soundly, knowing she'd all but pulled off a picture-perfect retirement party, but Mari knew the odds of closing her eyes for even a cat nap before her father's official announcement were slim, if not totally nonexistent.

So there she was, alone in her expansive living quarters, pacing up and down the length of her bedroom at three a.m., having long given up on the idea of rest. There were only two more hours before her alarm would go off, and the only thing stopping her from going downstairs to make herself a cappuccino and start her day was the fact that the rest of the household was still fast asleep. Sound carried through the tall ceilings and the ancient pipes, and she didn't want to subject everyone to her insomnia just because she was filled with nerves.

The changing light in the window was what first caught Marigold's eye. She'd been waiting for the dawn, but this was too early, and the light was too flickery to be the sun. Then, through the small opening of her window where she liked to let the breeze flow in, she heard a man's voice, or thought she did.

Her first thought went to Ryan, but what business did

he have in the garden at that hour? By the way she sometimes caught him looking at her, she wouldn't be entirely surprised to find him pulling a Romeo, but she thought he had more professional sense than that. *What light through yonder window breaks?* Then she parted the curtains and her whole body froze in place.

The garden – her mother's beautiful artwork of a garden, her pride and joy – was glowing orange and white as fire gobbled up everything in sight, growing larger by the second. Mari's mouth dropped open and her legs might have given way if her knees weren't locked. The tables and chairs, her pretty string lights, and most importantly, the garden itself was burning.

And there was a man standing just beyond the light of the flames, watching.

She saw the red gas cans at his feet first, and then the silhouette of his legs in a wide stance, his hands shoved in the pockets of a dark jacket. Recovered from her initial shock, she screamed at him from the window, but of course that only made him turn and run off toward the driveway. In a blind panic, Mari ran out of her bedroom and flew down the two flights of stairs to the garden, clutching her robe around her as she went.

"Fire!" she yelled as she ran past the staff quarters, then dashed toward the garden.

She paused inside for just a second, her heart thudding in her chest, and grabbed an umbrella from the stand near the door. It was the only thing within reach and she couldn't imagine herself actually using it to defend herself, but she wasn't about to let that man get away with this.

When she got to the garden, though, there was no one to wave the umbrella at. The man had made his escape, leaving his gas cans and all her beautiful flowers engulfed in fire.

"No, no, *no*," she cried as a lifetime of careful tending and nurturing went up in flames, not to mention all the hard work for her father's retirement party.

If it all burns to the ground, I'll be stuck with Ryan forever.

The thought was a little out of place, a little ridiculous, but it spurred her into action. She dropped the umbrella and shrugged out of her robe. It was a thin silk one that only came down to her upper thighs, but she'd seen plenty of people in movies using their clothes to smother fires. It was all she had, and all her brain was capable of coming up with in that frantic moment.

She threw the robe over the first flaming lily that she saw. It snuffed out the fire a lot better than she'd expected, blackening the robe and saving at least part of the flower. It was hot when she picked up the fabric, intent on doing the same thing to the next flaming plant.

"Ouch," she hissed, turning her face away from the heat and tossing her robe over a smoking tiger lily.

"Oh my god! What happened?"

Mari turned to see Emily running up the path, trying not to trip as her enormous, fuzzy slippers kicked gravel all over the place. Her eyes were as big as saucers and Mari had just enough self-awareness to know that the look of surprise wasn't a hundred percent due to the fire. She must look crazy standing out here in nothing but a short white nightgown, fighting the flames with her robe.

"I don't know," she said, moving on to the next flower. It was an exercise in futility. For every plant she saved – if half-burned and limp could even be considered *saved* – there were twenty more catching fire. "Call 911, Em."

"I already did," she said. "Come on, this is too dangerous-"

"I can't stand here and do nothing," Mari objected, stepping out of Emily's reach as she tried to pull her away from the fire. She dropped her robe on top of another plant. The fire ate away at it a little more with every attempt she made to salvage her garden, and by now it was looking more like Swiss cheese than imported silk.

"Okay, I'll get the garden hose," Emily said when she noticed the desperation in Mari's eyes. "Was this an accident?"

"No," Marigold said. "It definitely wasn't."

She pointed to the two gas cans at the end of the tables – what was left of them – and then she picked up her singed robe and moved on to the next plant.

❄

BY THE TIME the fire engines screamed their way into the gravel lot, Marigold and Emily were losing the war against the fire. Mari's beautiful silk robe was nothing but a burnt rag, the garden hose had proved almost entirely ineffective, and they were both covered in soot. As more of the staff came outside, Mari had tried to organize a bucket brigade, but when the firefighters arrived and ushered everyone else away from the fire, Mari found herself alone in the garden.

She refused to stand down, refused to let the fire win. Despite Emily's objections – and those of the firefighters themselves – she needed to keep trying. This wasn't just a collection of flowers. She knew every single plant in the garden, its origin and history. As she watched each one of them burn, it was like a funeral pyre.

Again.

And again.

And again.

"Miss Grimm?" one of the firefighters said. "If you'll just go stand with the others, we'll take it from here."

He took her by the shoulders before she could object, leading her forcefully out of the garden and delivering her to Emily. Em put her arms around Mari, holding her in place and trying in vain to comfort her, but all Mari saw were the orange flames destroying everything she cared about.

And then she saw the heavy hoses that the firefighters uncoiled from their trucks. They were careless, letting them drag through the remains of her garden. She watched someone turn on the water and then the high-powered spray started blowing what was left of her flowers straight off their stems.

Marigold let out a high-pitched yelp and Emily held her tighter as she watched her last hopes of salvaging the retirement party get washed away. Everything that wasn't ruined in the fire or withered from the gasoline was drowning in a torrent of water. Mari felt tears welling in the back of her throat. She knew how unhinged she must look in her soot-covered nightgown, but she refused to sacrifice the last shreds of her dignity by crying.

"We'll rebuild," Emily said, patting Mari's arm. "Don't worry."

"Rebuild in twelve hours?" she asked. "I don't think so."

Emily sighed and put her head on Marigold's shoulder, then suggested gently, "We'll postpone the party to another night. That's all."

That's all. Marigold took a deep breath, still valiantly fighting the urge to cry as her hopes and dreams died quietly inside her. Emily was right – of course she was. As the firefighters did their job and the fire slowly waned, Mari could see the true destruction that horrible man had wrought. Everything she and the staff had worked so hard to set up was ruined, and even if they managed to replace it all before this evening, the garden was all but unsalvageable.

"Oh my god," she said, breaking free of Emily's grasp and running back into the garden. She put her hand on the arm of the nearest firefighter and begged, "Can you please be careful? That's a Cinderella milkweed and you have no idea what I had to go through to get it."

She had the urge to dive in front of the flower, but luckily, she didn't have to. The firefighter – a woman whose steely eyes stood out from her bulky, soot-covered uniform – lowered her hose and sprayed the flower indirectly until the flames died with a hiss.

"Thank you," Marigold said. "I really appreciate your help – I don't mean to seem ungrateful, but your crew is devastating my garden."

The woman looked at her. It was more than a simple appraisal – her gray eyes sparkled with a curiosity that made Marigold very self-conscious of her outfit, or lack thereof. And was there recognition there as well? Mari narrowed her eyes at the woman – she looked familiar, but couldn't place her. Mari didn't know her in a professional capacity, and she didn't have much of a social life to speak of. A childhood acquaintance, then?

"Guys!" the woman said, cupping her hand around her mouth to shout at the rest of her crew, scattered throughout the garden. "Let's have a little finesse, okay? Try not to kill the plants any more than necessary!"

Marigold's heart melted at the gesture and she watched with relief as the rest of the crew pointed their hoses higher instead of blasting the water straight at her flowers.

"Thank you so much," she said.

"You're welcome," the woman answered. A little smile touched the corner of her lips, and then she nodded to where Emily and the rest of the staff was standing. "You should go back over there until the fire's out. Wouldn't want you to get wet."

Was that a little smirk Mari saw? And did her eyes flick ever so briefly down to Marigold's nightgown? She felt naked and embarrassed, and just a little bit excited. It must have been a stress reaction, her body's way of taking her mind off the fact that this was the worst night of her life.

She walked back over to Emily, at the very least relieved that she'd been able to stop the death-by-water of her remaining plants. And then it hit her – the woman was Cynthia Robinson, who moved to Grimm Falls when Marigold was fifteen, captured her attention at an ice cream parlor, and had been giving Mari the cold shoulder ever since.

NINE
CYN

Cyn couldn't get Marigold Grimm out of her head ever since she responded to the Grimm House fire, and it wasn't just because of that scandalously tiny nightgown she'd been wearing. Granted, if she'd been a betting woman, Cyn wouldn't have put money on Marigold owning a piece of clothing like that, but what most intrigued her was the new side to Marigold that she'd seen this morning.

She'd never been anything but perfectly poised and meticulously made up - never a hair out of place or an uncalculated response. But when Cyn's fire truck pulled into the gravel lot, there was Marigold, swatting frantically at the flames with the tattered remnants of what must have been a very expensive robe. Her ordinarily perfect blonde curls were frizzy and wild, there were smudges of soot on her arms and legs, and even a streak of it on the tip of her nose.

Frankly, she'd been a hot mess, and Cyn had never

seen her so emotional about anything. It scared her, lifting Marigold's carefully constructed mask and seeing fragility beneath it. That was why Cyn barked at her crew to take more pride in their work, and it was what stuck with Cyn long after they'd returned to the firehouse.

"I'm serious," she was saying to her crew while they sat around the break room table and wrote up their reports for the fire inspector. "Have you ever seen her lose her cool before? Nothing shakes her."

Well, nothing until this morning.

James rolled his eyes at her. "You know you haven't shut up about Marigold Grimm since four a.m.?"

"Yes I have," Cyn said defensively, but the rest of the guys shook their heads.

"No, Cinders, you haven't," James said. "Meanwhile, the rest of us are trying to figure out what a painting, a barn, and Grimm House have in common."

"You think all the fires are related?" she asked. It was mostly a rhetorical question – it was statistically unlikely that so many intentional fires could be set by different people in a city of this size at such short intervals.

"It's looking like we've got a serial arsonist on our hands," he said with a nod. "Now it's up to Holt to put the pieces together."

Cyn tapped her pencil against her paper. She'd been working on her report for the last hour and having trouble concentrating. The juxtaposition of innocent white silk and a scandalously short hem caressing Marigold Grimm's thighs just kept popping into her head, and she had to chase the image away again and again.

"'Two gas cans, empty, left at scene,'" she read from her report. "'Homeowner spotted a man in all black fleeing the premises.' Is that all we've got to go on?"

"And the cigarette butt," Gleeson added. "A partially smoked Winston that may or may not have belonged to the perp."

"Grimm House is always immaculate," James said. "There's no way it was dropped by a guest or staff member, especially with an event coming up."

Cyn nodded. She nibbled the eraser end of her pencil for a minute, then stood up and said, "Everybody done with your reports? I'll walk them over to the police station before I go on my lunch break."

She left the reports on Detective Holt's desk, then went down the street to The Magic Bean café, which kept her loaded with caffeine through many a long shift at the firehouse and which happened to have a pretty good food menu, too.

While she was standing in line to order, her mind went once again back to Marigold and Grimm House, and she had a sudden urge to head back over there. *Just to make sure I didn't miss any pertinent details in my report,* she thought. It was crazy to think that her quiet, friendly city was under attack, and she was determined to do everything in her power to nail the criminal before he could do any more damage.

If she found an opportunity to say a few more words to Marigold Grimm in the process, so much the better.

Cyn ordered two coffees instead of one, and after a moment's deliberation, she got a turkey sandwich and a ham sandwich – if Marigold's state this morning was any indication, she probably hadn't taken time to eat yet, and Cyn would give her dibs on the lunchmeat of her choosing.

Cyn was feeling anxious and second-guessing herself by the time she drove up the gravel drive to Grimm House, tucked away behind a large, wooded property. Coming back to double-check her work would seem insecure, or even incompetent. Coming back with a lunch for two when Marigold barely knew she existed – was she nuts?

But Cyn couldn't stop thinking about how devastated Marigold had been that morning, and more importantly, how their eyes had locked when she ran over to Cyn and begged her to be more careful with the water. It had made her heart stop, and when it started again, she was sure there had been a spark.

As unlikely as it seemed, Cyn just couldn't get the idea out of her head that Marigold Grimm had checked her out.

So she mustered every ounce of courage in her body – more than she'd ever needed to run into a burning building – and she got out of her truck with coffee and sandwiches in hand.

"Whoa."

The garden was in a surprising state of activity. There were at least a dozen people sorting through the burned and waterlogged mess outside and carrying what they could salvage into the house. Now that she saw it, Cyn realized she'd been imagining Marigold sitting there by herself, but she was Grimm Falls royalty. Of course she would have droves of people leaping to help her.

Cyn was there now, though, and she'd feel even more foolish if she just climbed back into her truck and left. So she carried her woefully insufficient two cups of coffee and her sandwich bag into the garden and asked the first person she saw, "Do you know where I can find Marigold Grimm?"

The woman glanced at Cyn's navy blue fire department t-shirt, then asked, "Is everything okay?"

"Oh yeah," Cyn said, then decided to stick with her original excuse for coming here. "I wanted to take another look at the grounds to make sure I didn't miss any clues about the fire this morning."

"Help yourself," the woman said. "Mari's in the flower garden trying to save what she can."

Cyn thanked her, then found her way to a more secluded part of the garden where Marigold was crouched over a partially-burned bed of her namesake flowers, her back to Cyn. There was police tape strung across the entrance to the burned area, but Marigold had ignored it, and so did Cyn.

As she approached, she noticed that Marigold had changed into a pair of jeans, dirty and wet around the hems, and a plain white t-shirt that clung to her back with the sweat of exertion. It betrayed the sinewy curves of her back, and Cyn cleared her throat to get her attention before she had a chance to stare too long.

"Marigold?"

"Yes?" she asked over her shoulder, then turned around. "Oh, it's you."

Cyn cast her eyes down to the gravel. "I'm sorry, I shouldn't have bothered you."

"Are you serious?" Marigold asked. "You're my hero."

She stood and looked at her dirty hands for a moment before giving up and wiping them on the thighs of her jeans. Cyn didn't expect that, nor did she expect the fact that Marigold's hair was still just as wild now as it had been at three in the morning. She'd tied it back with a ribbon, but she certainly wasn't her normal, impeccably groomed self.

Marigold extended her hand with a very disarming smile, and Cyn was feeling very uncertain about this whole misguided visit.

She clumsily juggled the coffees and sandwich bag in her hands, and after a moment of awkwardness that went on for a couple of beats too long, she gave up on shaking Marigold's hand and instead pressed one of the coffee cups into it. "I brought you coffee. And a sandwich. I figured you'd be hungry and exhausted, but it looks like you've got plenty of energy."

Stop talking. You're blathering.

She shut her mouth and smiled, waiting. Then Marigold returned the smile.

"That's really sweet of you. You came all the way here to bring me some coffee?"

"And a sandwich," Cyn said. "I got both turkey and ham so you could choose, but I didn't realize you'd have such a big staff. I should have brought more." *There you go again...* She changed the subject. Gesturing at the staff working around them, she asked, "Is the event still on for tonight?"

"It has to be," Marigold said, her tone becoming fiery and passionate. "I can't stand the idea of letting some anonymous *monster* ruin an event I've been planning for months. It won't be quite as grand as I originally envisioned, and I want to cry every time I think about how long it'll take to repair the damage to the garden, but it could have been a lot worse if it wasn't for you and your crew. Thanks for being so understanding – I must have seemed like a lunatic."

Cyn waved away the idea. "Not at all. Just last week I was consoling a hysterical museum director when one of his paintings was burned. Grief makes people react in ways they never predicted."

"Grief," Marigold said with a sad smile. "That's so appropriate. Did you know this was my mother's garden? It's sort of a memorial to her."

"Yes, I know," Cyn said. Most people in Grimm Falls were aware of the history behind the town, and all the elementary school kids had been on a field trip or two to Grimm House. But Cyn had heard it directly from Marigold a decade ago. "You probably don't remember me, but we hung out at the ice cream parlor a few times when we were kids. My stepmother used to force my stepbrother to bring me with him when he went, and you made it much more enjoyable."

Her heart stopped once again as she waited to find

out if those details jogged Marigold's memory at all. She should have left the past in the past – what if Marigold had no clue what she was talking about? Worse, what if she remembered and didn't care?

But Marigold smiled and said, "Yes, I remember you. Cynthia Robinson, the enigmatic girl from out of town, who rarely smiled but had an affinity for brightly-colored ice creams, and who, if memory serves, iced me out completely after about three weeks."

She was giving Cyn a challenging look – a flirtatious one? – and it left her speechless.

"I iced *you* out?" she asked. "You sent my stepbrother to tell me that you didn't want to be seen with me anymore."

Marigold furrowed her brow and asked, "Who's your stepbrother?"

"Drew Zeller," Cyn said. "He was in your grade in school. He said you thought I was annoying and clingy, so I did my best to leave you alone."

Mari frowned. "I never said that. I was intrigued by you, maybe even a little intimidated, but definitely not annoyed."

Cyn felt the words burning into her chest. *I was intrigued by you.* The words were hot and tingly, and they made absolutely no sense. For the last ten years, she pined over a girl who wanted nothing to do with her... and it was all based on a lie?

"You never said that?" she asked, dumbfounded.

"No," Marigold said with a frown. "Your stepbrother sounds like a jerk, Cynthia."

"He's complicated," Cyn said. It was the nicest word she could think of for Drew. "And it's Cyn, please. Or Cinders, but pretty much the only people who call me that are my work friends."

"Fine, then you can call me Mari," Marigold replied.

The possibility of spontaneously combusting from all the conflicting thoughts and emotions pin balling around in her head was very real, so Cyn changed the subject. Looking around, she said, "Your poor garden. How are you going to make the event happen?"

Cyn and her crew had done the best they could to put the fire out quickly, but there was so much devastation. The chairs were soaking wet, half the tables were burned, and apart from the plants that had been consumed by the fire and water, there were quite a few that had been doused in gas and doomed to shrivel up and die over the next couple of days.

"It's just going to have to move inside," Mari said with a sigh. "I was really looking forward to having the party in the garden. It might sound a little crazy, but I thought it would be a nice way to feel like my mother was present. But we'll use the ballroom and it'll be okay."

"I'm sure it will be beautiful," Cyn said, feeling a little tongue-tied again. Every time Marigold spoke, she was drawn to her plump lips, the teasing glimpses of her tongue sending little jolts of electric desire through Cyn's body.

She hadn't been this physically near Marigold since they were kids, and she was still struggling to process the possibility that Drew was the only thing standing between them all this time. She knew he'd harbored a crush on Marigold all through school, but was he really so protective of his life pre-Cyn that he would lie to prevent her first friendship in Grimm Falls?

Probably.

Cyn realized that she'd been staring into Marigold's diamond blue eyes too long and she blurted, "I want to help. Put me to work on clean-up duty."

Even as she made the offer, part of Cyn's brain clicked back over to practical matters and she realized she must be overdue to return from her lunch break. She wasn't about to rescind her offer, though. She was afraid that if she walked away now, she'd never have another excuse to see Marigold.

"No, you've already done more than enough," Mari said. Cyn's heart began to sink, but then Marigold's mouth twitched into a grin as she said, "In fact, you should come to the party. Are you free tonight?"

"Yes, but-"

"Good," Mari said. "It's the least I could do to thank you for helping save what we could of the garden. Please come."

Food was the last thing on Cyn's mind. Her heart was racing and she was dying to say yes, and yet something held her back. Fear? She'd been wanting to get close to Marigold Grimm for almost half of her life – what if Gus was right and the most likely outcome was heartbreak? Even worse, what if Cyn was reading all the signals right, but when Mari got to know her, she decided Cyn wasn't good enough for her after all?

"Marigold?" someone called from the house – a man's voice that made Mari stand a little taller when she heard it. "What's going on here?"

"That's my father," she explained to Cyn. "I need to go break the news about the garden. Will you come tonight?"

"Okay," Cyn said. She might be terrified, but in the end, there was no way she'd reject an opportunity to get closer to Marigold.

"Good," she said. "I look forward to seeing you."

Then she surprised Cyn, taking a quick step forward and putting her arms around Cyn's neck to hug her. That's when Cyn's brain short-circuited. She turned her head in the same moment that Mari did, both of them going to the right, and their lips met accidentally.

For a brief and unbelievable second, every nerve ending in Cyn's body came alive and she'd never felt anything quite like it. No adrenaline rush, no fire engine siren, no burning building could compare to the soft, faintly honey-flavored kiss that she and Marigold shared.

And then Mari stepped back with a nervous giggle and Cyn said, "Sorry."

"No, I am. I'm a hugger," Mari said, clearly flustered.

"Hey, that's one way to thank someone," Cyn said.

She earned another little chuckle from Marigold, and then Mari's father called her again from the doorway. Mari said, "I'll see you tonight?"

"You bet," Cyn said. Then Mari rushed away and Cyn realized she was still holding the sandwich bag. She wasn't hungry anymore – maybe James would take them off her hands when she got back to the firehouse.

She watched Mari duck under the caution tape and head for the house at a brisk pace, then Cyn wandered back to her car with her head in the clouds, completely disinterested in her coffee lest it take away the taste of honey on her lips.

TEN
MARIGOLD

Mari was grateful for the excuse to high-tail it out of that embarrassing moment. Cyn was an attractive woman and Marigold couldn't deny noticing the way her biceps moved beneath the snug sleeves of her t-shirt, or the way her short, chestnut hair fell seductively over her eyes at times.

But she wasn't the type of girl to go around acting on impulse or giving in to her desires, especially when there was so much work to be done and more important things to think about. That kiss had been a confusing, exciting and strange accident, and she was happy to put it out of her mind.

"Hi, Dad," she said as she joined her father on the terrace just outside the kitchen. She had a sudden urge to hold her arms out in a t-shape, as if she could shield him from the catastrophe behind her. "Did Emily call you?"

Mari sure hadn't. If she'd had her way, he would show up tonight at six p.m. in his tuxedo, the event would be set up indoors, and aside from the change in location, he'd have no idea anything happened at all. She could fill him in on the fire and the possible arson *after* he congratulated her on an event well-executed and handed the reins over to her.

But here he was, his eyes wide as he looked over her head to all the staff members carrying soggy chairs and half-burned tables out of the garden to be disposed of. "She did – she told me there was a fire early this morning. What happened?"

Marigold put her hand to her hair. She did her best to run her fingers through it, tucking it neatly into the ribbon that held it back as she explained – some people would call it lying. "It was a small fire, and the fire truck got here quickly to put it out. The tables and chairs are ruined, and so are some of Mom's flowers. But I've already started setting up new tables in the ballroom – your retirement party will go off without a hitch."

She was pleased with herself. That sounded like a pretty minor hiccup in the plans, and she hoped to keep steering the conversation away before her father had a chance to dig deeper.

"If you want to come back inside with me, I'll show you where your table will be-"

"Emily told me it was an act of violence," he said, stopping her in her tracks. Her father could be immovable when he wanted to be – a trait she admired, and one she still hadn't figured out how to work with. "I believe the word 'arson' was used."

Mari let out a sigh. *Thanks, Em.*

"It was," she confessed. "I saw a man in the garden when it happened, but he didn't look familiar. He ran before I could stop him, and I don't know why he did it."

She hated that fact even more than she hated having to adapt the beautiful event she had planned. Uncertainty was not something she readily accepted in any aspect of her life, least of all when it concerned Grimm House.

"We have to cancel the party," her father said. "If there's a criminal running around with unknown motives, we can't risk another incident with a house full of people."

Marigold's heart sank into her gut. She knew he was only being pragmatic, but she'd been fighting people who wanted to cancel the event since four this morning and she was exhausted. Was that why Emily had called him, to force Marigold to call off the party?

"No," she said. "I've put too much work into planning this event, and I've been busting my butt to do damage control for the last eight hours. There won't be another incident tonight because the guy chose the middle of the night to set his fire – he obviously doesn't want to hurt anyone. And if he shows up, we'll have people from both the police and fire departments in attendance, as well as private security. You deserve your retirement party, Dad."

And I deserve my turn at the wheel, she thought, hating how selfish it felt to think about that right now.

"Okay, princess," her father said with a resigned sigh. "This is your event, so it's your call."

Then to her surprise, he pulled her into a hug. She couldn't remember the last time he'd done that – a real hug, and not just a shorthand *I love you* squeeze of her shoulder. She probably should have been embarrassed – especially because when she looked over her father's shoulder, she caught Cyn glancing at her on her way to her truck. But instead, she just accepted the hug.

"I'm so sorry to hear about the garden," he said. "I don't care how much it costs, we'll get the landscapers in here on Monday to replace everything, down to the very last flower."

He released her, and it should have been a comforting thought, but instead it made Marigold feel cold to think of a crew of strangers digging up and replanting her mother's garden. "Thanks, but I think I'd like to start the process myself. Should we go inside and make sure everything's the way you want it?"

"Sure," her father said. As they walked through the kitchen, he looked around dramatically and asked, "And where the hell is Ryan? Why isn't he helping?"

"Umm," Mari hedged, glancing down at the highly-polished floor, "I haven't told him yet. He's downtown, dropping in on all the vendors to finalize details and pick up some last-minute table settings."

"Oh, now, that's ridiculous," her father chastised Mari. "I know you don't like relying on anyone. You've got a stubborn streak a mile wide, but it's not a sign of weakness to delegate tasks. Besides, he's a director – he has a right to know what's going on. Go call him, right now."

Marigold swallowed.

If her father was feeling affectionate earlier, that moment had passed. She hadn't heard such a booming paternal command since she was in high school and she announced over the dinner table that she intended to enroll at Grimm Falls College so she could help run the estate, rather than apply to the Ivy League schools her father wanted her to attend. *Go to your room and finish your Harvard essay right now, young lady.*

Yes, sir.

"Yes, sir."

She left her father in the ballroom, where a more traditional array of round tables was being set up all around the room and slip covers were being put onto chairs at a rapid rate. The clock was ticking and everything was coming together remarkably well... so why did Ryan need to be part of it?

Mari went out to the foyer and took the grand staircase up to the second floor where her office sat right next to her father's. She knew he was right – even though she didn't want to share the estate with him, Ryan deserved to be kept abreast of developments here so he could do his job. And he did it well – it was just that she and Ryan had fundamentally different ideas about the way the estate should be run, and whether history or profit was most important.

She glanced into her father's office on her way past. The large, ornate doors were always open – a policy she planned to keep once the room became hers. Everything else about it, though, would have to go. The office was enormous and ostentatiously decorated, with a desk the size of a Cadillac right in the center of it all.

Marigold planned to keep the desk, a hand-carved piece from Germany that her great-grandfather brought with him when Grimm House was built, but she'd slide it into one corner and use the rest of the large room for meeting space.

For now, she went into her own office, still large but much more modestly decorated. She hardly spent any time here, but the rest of the house was bustling with activity at the moment and she didn't want to have this grudging conversation in earshot of her father. She picked up the phone on her desk and dialed Ryan's number instead of using her cell phone to maintain a professional distance.

While she waited for him to answer, she stretched the long cord over to the big picture window behind the desk. She hadn't looked at the garden from above since last night, and at first, she was afraid to see the damage.

There was a big black patch where everything had been turned to ash and soot, like a meteor had come and obliterated a quarter acre of her beautiful garden. From up here, though, it didn't look quite so bad as it did up close. There was still plenty of untouched green around it, and that lifted Marigold's spirits a little.

"Mari?"

She clenched her teeth. She wasn't fond of Ryan using her nickname, and sometimes when he got too familiar, she had to bite back the request to be addressed as *Miss Grimm*. She stood a little taller and put on a fake smile for the benefit of her empty office, then said, "Hi, Ryan. I just wanted to let you know there was a fire here last night, but I've got everything under control-"

"A fire?" he asked. "What do you mean?"

Marigold let out a sigh, careful not to let the receiver pick it up, then repeated the whole thing to him, just like she had explained it to her father. Ryan was angry, especially when she told him it happened over eight hours ago. All in all, the conversation went a lot less smoothly than the one she'd had with her father.

"You should have told me when it happened," he said. "I would have come right away and helped you."

"Well, I'm telling you now," Mari said, feeling guilty and petulant all at once. Then she added another little white lie to the stack and said, "There's been a lot going on this morning and I just didn't have the time."

"You could have asked Emily to call me," Ryan said.

"You're right," she said. "I'm sorry. Can you please go to the florist's before you come here and see what she can do about replacing the white tulips that were ruined?"

"Of course," Ryan said. "I'm happy to help."

"Thank you," she said, then they hung up. His eagerness to help made her feel guilty for being so determined to shut him out, but she was no less determined to personally see to the success of this event.

She went to the window again after she replaced the phone receiver in its cradle, and glanced down at the area of the garden where she and Cyn had spoken. Even though it was blackened and horrible, Mari found something to smile about. She put her fingertips to her bottom lip, remembering their accidental kiss.

ELEVEN
CYN

Cyn ended up being more than half an hour late returning from her lunch break, and the guys at the firehouse enjoyed ribbing her about her impromptu trip to Grimm House all afternoon. She didn't mind, though, and she just let them tease her because she had a golden ticket – an invitation to the party and a chance to see Marigold again.

Mari, she'd said. *You can call me Mari.*

The words – and that kiss – kept running through Cyn's mind and bringing a smile to her lips. She wanted to tell herself she was being silly, that it was all in her head, and that the spark she felt that morning when Marigold ran up to her and grabbed her arm was imagined. She wanted to tell herself it was all a lie, because there would be no need for bravery in that case.

But it wasn't.

The lie was what Drew had told her when they were kids.

Cyn had been making friends with Marigold a little more each time they met at the ice cream parlor. Back then, everything in her life was in flux – she was in a new town, living with a new family who didn't seem to like her much, about to start a new school, and her dad never wanted to talk about her mother's death, or her life for that matter. But Marigold was a silver lining – one thing that made all the rest bearable.

Her mom had passed, too, so she could relate to something that no one else in Cyn's life understood. Plus, she was pretty, smart, and she made Cyn smile when she thought that part of herself had been irrevocably broken.

That's why it hurt so much when Drew delivered the news that Marigold didn't want anything to do with her. Cyn was too young, too clingy, too obviously crushing on her while Marigold had no interest in her.

Had *any* of it been true?

Cyn made a quick pit stop at Green Thumb Nursery after work, then went back to the carriage house to get ready for the party. The evening seemed to stretch on forever – a limbo state in which Marigold Grimm both was and wasn't returning her interest after all these years of yearning. Cyn got dressed, selecting a crisp black suit with a white button-up shirt. She considered a tie, but then she left the top two buttons open as Samantha's voice began unexpectedly swimming around her head.

You should wear the gold chain from two Christmases ago, Cyn could hear her, clear as if she was looking over her shoulder. *Just a little bling to make you stand out.*

Right, like a bird plumping its feathers for a mating

dance, Cyn thought, but then she went over to her jewelry box and took out the gold chain she'd been thinking of. *Girls like Marigold do like a little sparkle.* She lay the gold chain over her crisp, white collar, then she slipped her feet into a pair of Italian leather loafers – one of the few items from Samantha's boutique that Cyn had received as a gift and actually drooled over beforehand. She didn't have many occasions to wear them, but she always kept them immaculately polished and tucked safely at the back of her closet.

She walked back over to the mirror for one last check, slipping and sliding along the way. The soles of her loafers were so unmarred with use that she had to take a minute to get her bearings whenever she wore them.

I'll bring a pair of sneakers just in case, she thought. Then, satisfied that she looked as good as she was going to get, she headed out the door.

❄

CYN WAS FILLED with nervous energy by the time she arrived at Grimm House a little past eight o'clock, with the potted plant she'd picked up at Green Thumb tucked under her arm. It was a silly gesture – who brought anything but cut flowers to a woman like Marigold Grimm?

She was feeling self-conscious about the plant as she walked into the house, stepping carefully so as not to slip in her loafers. She was truly a fish out of water as she looked around at the people in tuxedos and ball gowns standing in clusters, chatting and drinking from expensive champagne flutes. Cyn wondered whether Mari had actually meant to extend an invitation to her, or if it had merely been politeness that made her ask.

She was here now, though. The fingers of her free hand went reflexively to the gold chain on her neck as she headed for the ballroom to the right of the grand staircase.

The ballroom was very large, with ceilings at least twenty feet high and intricate woodwork all around. There were about two dozen round tables scattered around the room, with perfectly crisp, white tablecloths and meticulous place settings. Each one was an elegant pop of gold, with crystal water goblets and tangerine-colored tulips tucked into the cloth napkins.

There was a bar at one end of the room, where a number of guests had gathered to sip cocktails, and a string quartet played softly in front of an as-yet empty dance floor. Cyn craned her neck to look for Marigold, but there were at least a hundred people in the room. She looked for Drew – any familiar face would be welcome – and when her eye caught Detective Holt's, she was grateful as he waved her over to his table.

"Robinson," he said with a surprised smile. "What are you doing here?"

"Marigold Grimm asked me to come," she said, and it sounded even more improbable out loud. Maybe it *had* just been a polite invitation, and Mari would be even more surprised to see her than Holt was. "I responded to the fire this morning and made sure my guys didn't do any more damage to the garden than we had to."

"Well, we have an extra chair - you should join us," Holt said, putting his arm around a pretty woman in a black velvet slip dress. "This is my wife, Donna. Frank's around here somewhere, and the police chief. Have a seat."

Cyn nodded. Frank was the fire chief, and she'd met the police chief a few times as well. If nothing else came of tonight, a little elbow-rubbing with her superiors wouldn't be such a bad thing. She shook Donna's hand, a little too rough because she was used to having to hold her own against the guys at the firehouse. Then she sat down and a waiter came around to fill her water goblet.

"What are you drinking?" Holt asked, nodding toward the bar.

"Oh, I don't drink," Cyn said. Holt arched an eyebrow, so she added, "Bad experience as a teenager – it really put me off the stuff."

"To each his own," Holt said, tipping back a glass of dark amber liquor. Then he spotted the plant – delicate bluebells that reminded Cyn of Marigold's eyes – and asked, "What's up with the plant?"

"Umm, it's a hostess gift," Cyn said, fighting off the urge to blush. She took the pot off the table and tucked it carefully beneath her chair, then just to change the conversation, she asked, "Have you made any progress in the arson case?"

"Since this morning?" he snorted. "Nope."

"What about the other incidents? The painting and the barn?" she pressed.

"Cinders," she heard a familiar voice chastising her. "Did you come all the way out here to bug Holt about a work matter?"

She turned to see Frank, her boss. He was holding a stein of frothy beer, and the police chief and both of their wives stood beside him. Cyn shook her head, color rising into her cheeks. "No, I'm sorry. Marigold invited me."

"No need to apologize," he said as he pulled out a chair for his wife, then threw Cyn a wink. "But if you're going to pull off a feat like that, then try to enjoy your night off. Relax and quit talking about fires."

"Yes, sir," she said.

She settled into a slightly fidgety silence, running her thumb over the uneven surface of her crystal goblet while her superiors remarked on the quality of the bourbon and their wives chatted in a way that made it clear they were old friends. They'd probably been coming to events like this for years.

Cyn didn't have to sit with her discomfort for long, though. She noticed Marigold the moment she walked into the ballroom, and everything else dulled in comparison.

She was wearing a blush pink, full-length gown with tulle that accentuated the curve of her hips. She was absolutely striking in white satin gloves that came up to her elbows and a thin satin choker around her delicate neck. Cyn didn't think she was imagining it when it seemed like every head in the room turned toward

Marigold, and she could have stolen the show if she'd walked into the ballroom in a burlap sack.

Or a singed silk nightgown, Cyn thought with a quick smile.

"She's something else, isn't she?" Frank said when he noticed the direction of her gaze. He laughed and turned to his wife as he added, "I'm surprised she's not wearing a tiara. They already call her Grimm Falls royalty, and she seems to like the title."

Cyn listened quietly while her table talked about how unapproachable Marigold Grimm was, all the while her eyes tracked her as she glided across the room, smiling a little too intentionally and saying hello to all the most important people. Cyn would have said the same about her before this morning – *detached, elitist, aloof* – but now she was beginning to think it was all an act.

"I'm going to say hello," she announced. "I want to thank her for the invitation."

Frank just raised his eyebrow at her, then turned his attention back to the police chief.

❄

CYN FOUND Drew on her way to Marigold. He was standing at the entrance to the ballroom and when she saw him, she made a quick detour to say hello – mostly because she hadn't yet built up the courage to talk to Mari.

"Drew," she said, catching his attention. "How's the security detail going? Any sign of trouble?"

"No," he said. "Just a lot of rich people eating caviar. The real question is what the hell are *you* doing here?"

"Marigold invited me," Cyn said.

Drew looked unimpressed with the invitation, then nodded at the plant under her arm. "What's that?"

"They're bluebells," Cyn explained. "A hostess gift."

"Geez, you still have a crush on Marigold Grimm after all these years, don't you?" Drew asked. "You know a plant in a plastic pot isn't going to impress her, right?"

He gestured at the opulence surrounding them and she figured he was right about that, but she hoped Mari would appreciate the meaning behind the gift. She shifted them to her other arm and said, "Speaking of Marigold, I had a very interesting conversation with her this afternoon. She said she never asked you to tell me to back off when we were kids. Why would you lie about something like that?"

Drew narrowed his eyes at her, then said, "I don't know what you're talking about."

"When I first moved to Grimm Falls," Cyn insisted, "I met Marigold at the ice cream parlor and after a couple of weeks, you said that she didn't want me around anymore and I should leave her alone. Drew, she was the only friend I had at the time and you drove a wedge between us."

"No, sorry," Drew said flippantly. "I don't remember that."

"I don't believe you."

"Here comes your girlfriend," Drew said, cutting Cyn off. He nodded over her shoulder and she turned around to see Marigold weaving her way through the crowd. She wasn't aiming for Cyn – more like circulating near her – but when Cyn turned around again, Drew had slipped into the crowd.

Cyn took a deep breath, then went to say hello to Marigold. She caught up with her just as Mari was plucking an hors d'oeuvre off a circulating waiter's shiny silver platter.

"Hi," Cyn said as she watched a juicy, bacon-wrapped fig disappear into Marigold's mouth. *I want to be that fig,* one half of her brain thought while the other scrambled to remember how to form words. "Umm, well it looks like you pulled it off. The ballroom looks beautiful."

"The tulips are tangerine instead of white, and the garden would have been such a pretty backdrop, but it all came together in the end," Mari said with a smile, those diamond blue eyes burning into Cyn's. "Did you doubt me?"

"No," Cyn said. "Not for a second."

"Thank you," Marigold said. Her eyes swept discretely over Cyn's clothes, settling on the gold chain at her neck. Cyn's heart was already in her throat, and it only climbed higher as Mari reached for the chain. She adjusted it – it had gotten tangled in Cyn's collar – and then her gloved hand lingered on Cyn's chest for just a second as she said, "You clean up well, Miss Firefighter."

"Did you doubt me?" Cyn asked, raising an eyebrow and daring to flirt. Now that she was standing in front of

Marigold, every doubt that she'd had melted away. There was chemistry between them, and it was strong.

Mari laughed and averted her eyes, landing on the bluebells under Cyn's arm. "What's that?"

"Oh," Cyn said, presenting them to her, "they're for you. I know cut flowers are more traditional, but I figured if you like them, you could plant them in the garden after the event. That way, maybe it'll feel like your mom's at the party with you after all?"

Every time she started to say something, Marigold had a way of making her second-guess herself. Was that the dumbest idea she'd ever come up with? She'd thought it was perfect when she was standing inside Green Thumb Nursery, thinking about what Mari had said about the significance of her garden, but now she wasn't sure. Marigold was just staring at her.

Then her eyebrows turned up, wrinkling in the most adorable way.

"That is the most thoughtful thing anyone's ever done for me," she said, taking the little plastic pot and throwing her arms around Cyn's neck. She was careful to keep her head turned this time – as much as she wanted to feel Marigold's lips on hers again, the middle of the crowded ballroom was hardly the place. Mari let her go, then inspected the plant. "These bluebells are going to be beautiful in the garden. Thank you so much."

Cyn stood a little taller, trying not to grin like an idiot. "You're welcome."

Mari looked toward the front of the room, where a podium had been set up to the left of the quartet. She checked the time on a delicate silver watch that hung over her long gloves, then said, "I'm really glad you came. I've got hostess duties to attend to, but I'd love to have a drink with you at some point tonight."

"How about a dance instead?" Cyn asked.

Mari looked sheepishly around the room. All of Grimm Falls' elite were here tonight, as well as major players from the local government. Was it asking too much to dance with Marigold in front of them all? Cyn held her breath, hoping she hadn't just screwed up her one and only opportunity to get to know Marigold Grimm.

"Unless you have a date who might object," she added quickly. "I didn't mean to be presumptuous."

"No, there's no date," Mari said. "I always go stag to these things – you're not the only one with fires to put out, but mine are thankfully the metaphorical type." She glanced at the clock again, then said, "I need to make my introductions and bring out the main course. Why don't you enjoy your meal, then I'll find you and we'll see about that dance?"

Those light blue eyes were even more vibrant and lovely than Cyn had remembered. She kept falling into them and losing her place in the conversation. She spoke with more confidence than she felt as she shot Mari a smile and said, "I'm looking forward to it."

She watched as Marigold picked her way to the front of the room, the volume of her dress making it look like she floated her way to the podium. Cyn headed back to the table with her boss and Detective Holt, and as she slid into her seat, Frank shot her an intrigued look. There would be questions at the firehouse tomorrow – probably a lot of them – but that was a small price to pay for this incredible evening.

Marigold set the bluebells carefully on the podium, then she found Cyn in the audience, their eyes locking for an instant. Then Marigold was in full-on hostess mode. She switched on a small microphone and welcomed everyone to her father's retirement party, then brought out the guest of honor to sit at a special table at the front of the room with her and a few other Grimm House staff members. Finally, she signaled a small army of waiters to come out of the kitchen with entrées stacked expertly on their arms.

Cyn enjoyed the best chicken paprikash she'd ever eaten and was doing her best to contribute to the conversation at her table even though she felt a little out of her depth. She tried not to look too often toward the front table, where Marigold sat primly, the tulle of her dress pluming up around her. Cyn watched as she took dainty bites of her chicken, alternating with sips of white wine. Everything Marigold did was so intentional, so practiced. Even the way she smiled looked rehearsed, and Cyn was dying to find out what lay beneath that perfect veneer.

TWELVE
MARIGOLD

Mari lost track of Cyn for a while. Sitting next to her father during dinner, with Ryan on her other side, she got absorbed in her thoughts about what her father might say when it was time for his speech at the end of the evening.

It was true that the party turned out just as well as she hoped, even with the not-so-little snag in her plans. And it was also true that she'd been managing various aspects of the estate since high school. But her father seemed bound and determined to saddle her with Ryan in the misguided belief that a business partner would make her life easier, or better somehow.

After the meal, Marigold was pulled into the kitchen to deal with a few questions the caterer had about the timing of dessert, and then she had several lengthy and painfully dry conversations with her father's favorite business associates.

By the time she found a moment to break away and

ask Cyn for that dance, the sizzling firefighter in the sharp black suit was nowhere to be found.

Did she leave?

Mari asked around, and when she found the fire chief at the bar with his wife, he pointed her into the foyer, saying, "I saw her heading for the door about a minute ago. Maybe she went out for some air."

Marigold walked briskly, unwilling to let tonight be another missed connection. She liked Cyn when they were kids – Cyn was a little too young for anything real to develop between them at the time, and then when she abruptly stopped talking to Marigold, she assumed it was for the same reason everyone else in Grimm Falls kept their distance from her. She was not ignorant of her nickname – *Grimm Falls royalty*.

But apparently that wasn't what had driven them apart all those years ago, and she wanted to know more.

Mari's heels clicked on the marble floor in the foyer. She probably hadn't sat down for more than an hour out of all her waking time in the last seventy-two hours – not counting the meal she'd just eaten, which came not a minute too soon. Still, she couldn't wait to get out of these heels at the end of the night – maybe even kick back and truly enjoy herself after her father's retirement announcement.

She found Cyn standing at the edge of the garden, her back to Marigold. The sound of the string quartet floated out through the open windows and Marigold had to try not to admire the view of Cyn's backside for too long.

"Hi," she said.

Cyn turned around and smiled. "You found me."

"I was hoping you hadn't left," Marigold said. "What are you doing out here?"

"Just looking at the scene of the crime," Cyn said. She flicked the yellow caution tape that was hanging at about hip height across the entrance to the garden. "Detective Holt said there haven't been any leads just yet, but I'm sure they're going to figure out who did this. I won't let them stop looking until they do."

"Thanks," Mari said as she joined Cyn in front of the tape. "I was hoping to get that dance now. The dance floor is filling up in there."

"Well, I wouldn't want to compete with a crowd," Cyn said, surprising her as she took Marigold's gloved hand and put her other hand on her waist, right where the tulle began to plume out.

"Here?" Mari asked, her breath catching in her throat. The garden was cast in shadows, just a few lamp posts lighting the features and a row of string lights illuminating the paths. Her heels were sinking into the gravel and it was painful to look at the charred remains of her garden, and yet when Cyn pulled her a little closer, she didn't object.

"Why not?" Cyn asked. "We can hear the music just as well here."

"Okay," Marigold said as Cyn began to turn her around in slow circles. Her heart was pounding and she couldn't tear her eyes off Cyn's steely gaze. Cyn was a few inches taller than Marigold and she wondered if she was the only one feeling the tension in that moment. It would be so easy to tilt her head up, rise ever so slightly onto her toes, and kiss her again.

"I talked to my stepbrother earlier," Cyn said. "He's working security here tonight, and he claims to have no memory of telling me that you didn't want to talk to me anymore."

"Do you believe him?" Marigold asked.

"No," Cyn said. "I think he had a crush on you."

"You'll have to point him out to me," Mari said.

"Why, so you can have your pick of us?" Cyn asked, a teasing smirk coming to her lips.

"No!" Marigold objected. "Believe me, I'm not interested. I just want to know if I remember him from school."

"Okay," Cyn said.

When the quartet paused between numbers, Cyn let go of Marigold and she found herself craving more. Everything was running smoothly inside the ballroom for the moment, so to linger in this moment a little longer, she asked, "Do you want to see my second favorite part of the estate?"

"Yes," Cyn said, her lip turning up to a charming half-smile as those steel-colored eyes studied Mari's face. She was lucky it was dark out here or Cyn would have seen the desire in her expression. One thing she couldn't disguise was the way her eyes lingered over Cyn's lips.

"Come on," Mari said, feeling brave and taking Cyn's hand.

They went back into the house and Mari guided her

quickly up the grand staircase before anyone could grab her and pull her back into the fray. They went to the second floor, where her great-grandfather's library waited. She let go of Cyn's hand to push the large doors open, then stepped aside.

Cyn's eyes lit up.

"Wow," she said, going into the room.

It was grand just like everything else in Grimm House, with mahogany bookshelves that went all the way up to the ceiling on three walls. Ladders were mounted to a rail system that circled the room, and small overhead lights illuminated each shelf.

Mari was pleased at the look of awe that had overcome Cyn's expression. She loved showing this room to people – it was a great judge of character, and she asked, "Do you like to read?"

Cyn turned around from the bookshelf where she was examining a row of leather-bound classics. "I love to read. Romances, mostly - I'm a bit of a sap."

Marigold grinned and said, "I never would have guessed."

"What about you? What do you read?" Cyn asked.

"Oh, these are just for show," Marigold said with a flick of her wrist. Cyn clutched her chest, her fingers tangling in the chain of her necklace, and Mari laughed, then relented. "I'm joking. I'm a classics girl – Hesse, Goethe, Remarque. A lot of the books in this library came over from Germany with my great-grandfather, and I've read all the ones that aren't too delicate to open."

"Oh, thank god," Cyn said, putting her hand back

down and walking a little closer to Marigold. *Sauntering?* "If you had all these books and told me you weren't a reader, I was going to have to go home and forget all about that kiss."

Mari laughed and pointed out, "It wasn't a kiss. It was an accident."

"Do you regret it?"

Cyn's eyes were smoldering into her and no, she absolutely did not regret their kiss. Marigold shook her head, nearly imperceptibly because she was afraid to break their gaze. That was all Cyn needed, though.

She smiled. "Then it was a kiss."

Our first, Marigold thought. What a crazy idea.

She went over to a comfortable, well-worn leather armchair that she'd spent many an hour in when she was growing up. When she sat down, Cyn grinned and pointed at the pink tulle that was ballooning all around her.

"I don't think you fit in that chair, honey," she said, and Marigold gave her a sharp look.

"Watch it," she said, but a smile played on her lips.

"I meant to say your dress doesn't," Cyn added, looking sufficiently chastised. "Which you look incredible in, by the way. True Grimm Falls royalty." Mari rolled her eyes and Cyn caught it. "Did I say something wrong?"

"No," Marigold said. "I just hear that a lot, and it's usually not a positive. It can be pretty isolating, actually."

"I know what that's like," Cyn said. She was closing the distance between them, pausing now and then to inspect something on the bookshelves – or pretend to – and all the while approaching the second leather chair right next to Mari's.

Finally, Marigold laughed and patted the arm of the chair. "Sit down. You're making me anxious."

"You don't have to get back to the party?"

"I will eventually," she said, then let out a groan and slipped her feet out of her heels. "But my feet are killing me, and I'm curious about why your stepbrother would tell you I didn't like you when we were kids. Is that what sibling rivalry is like?"

"I guess," Cyn said, obeying her order to sit. "We never got along – still don't, most of the time. Our parents got married pretty quickly and I think he blames me for stealing his mother's attention away from him."

"How did they meet?" Mari asked.

"An online grief support group," Cyn said.

"Your mother passed right before you came to Grimm Falls, right?"

"Yes, she had cancer and died when I was eleven," Cyn said. Then she reached down and lifted Marigold's foot onto her lap. She looked at her, waiting for an objection, but Mari said nothing, barely able to breathe. Cyn put her hands on her, rolling the balls of her thumbs into Marigold's arch and then massaging her heel.

Mari let out another moan as the pain that had been building in her feet for the last several days was released, and a new kind of wanting emerged. She settled deeper into the leather chair and lifted her other foot into Cyn's lap, their eyes never leaving each other as Cyn massaged her.

After a minute, she continued her story. "My mother didn't want my dad to pine over her for the rest of his life, so she made him promise to remarry when she was gone. Sometimes I think he chose Samantha just because she could understand what it was like to lose a spouse, but for better or worse, we've been in Grimm Falls ever since."

"I'm sorry. My mother died in childbirth," Marigold said. Then she gave a small, sad laugh and said, "Wow, that's a hell of a thing to have in common. So where did you live before?"

"A little town called Lisbon," she said. "It's about three hours from here – nothing but soybeans and Amish country surrounding it, and not a whole lot going on inside the town, either. It's the kind of place you see in Hallmark movies, where everyone knows each other and you can walk pretty much anywhere you want to go."

"That sounds idyllic," Marigold said. "Why didn't you and your father stay there?"

"Samantha's boutique was here," Cyn said with a shrug. "We couldn't really ask her to uproot her business to settle in a town where people were excited to finally have a Wal-Mart to call their own."

Marigold laughed. Then, watching the expert way Cyn worked her hands over her feet and up her calves a little way, she asked, "But you're happy here?"

"Yes," Cyn said, catching her gaze. "I love Grimm Falls. That's why this rash of arson attacks is bothering me so much – I can't believe anyone would want to do something like that to our city."

"I read about the other cases in the paper," Mari said. "Do you think my garden is related to them?"

"I don't understand the connection any more than you do," Cyn said, "But I would sleep better at night knowing we had one criminal on our hands instead of three."

"I'd sleep better at night if my mother's garden was still in one piece," Marigold said. "Thank you for the bluebells, though. It really meant a lot to me that you understood when I said I wanted my mother here tonight."

"I would never laugh at you," Cyn said, keeping her gaze steady on Marigold.

Then she released her feet, gently sliding them back into her heels and setting them on the floor. She stood and held out her hand and Mari took it, confused and excited all at the same time.

"Where are we going?" she asked as Cyn pulled her out of the chair.

She didn't make it any farther than Cyn's arms. She pulled her close and gave her a deep, intentional kiss. It felt like all the air in the room had been sucked out and replaced by something denser, more electrically charged.

When they parted a moment later, Mari asked, "What was that for?"

"I told you, I'm a romantic," Cyn said. "Wasn't it the right moment?"

"Yes," Mari breathed. "It was."

THIRTEEN
CYN

Cyn was making out with the woman of her dreams. *How the hell had that happened?!*

She had Marigold Grimm pressed up against a bookshelf. Her lips still tasted like honey, but now it was mixed with the sweet flavor of white wine and Cyn was going crazy with desire. She had her hands around Marigold's hips, trying not to mess up the tulle on her dress while she worked up the courage to slide her palms down to Mari's perfect ass.

It had taken all of her courage to go for that first kiss – or was it their second, considering what had happened in the garden? But after that, the gloves had come off, quite literally. Cyn had pulled those long, silky white gloves from Marigold's delicate fingers, and now her hands were cupped around Cyn's neck. Cyn had the recurring desire to pinch herself to make sure she wasn't dreaming, and she stole looks into Marigold's diamond blue eyes every chance she got.

This is happening. It's real. Marigold Grimm just wrapped her leg around my hip.

"I don't normally do this kind of thing," Mari said in between frantic, passionate kisses. One of her hands traveled over Cyn's collarbone and tripped over the gold chain on its way to the top button of her shirt.

"Me neither," Cyn said. She wanted to tell her she'd never consider doing this with anyone *but* her, but that seemed like too much, like she would scare Mari off. She would never forgive herself if she ruined this moment.

"I don't want you to think I go around kissing girls on a first date, or a... whatever this is," Mari kept objecting while she worked the buttons on Cyn's shirt. It emboldened Cyn to slide her own hands down, squeezing the surprising suppleness of Mari's ass through far too many layers of fabric.

"This isn't a date," she said. "You'll *know* when I take you on a date. We can stop if you want."

"No."

Thank god.

Mari wrapped her leg tighter around Cyn's body and she let herself lean into the feeling. Their hips connected just as Mari finished undoing the buttons of Cyn's shirt and spread it open. She was wearing an undershirt, and a bra beneath that, but it felt good to have one less layer between them as she pressed her body into Marigold's and kissed her again.

Mari was just sliding her hands into the narrow space between them, looking for the button of Cyn's pants, when something vibrated violently against her leg and they both jumped. Mari let out a startled yelp and Cyn stepped back, scrambling for her phone.

It was blaring now in addition to the vibration, an alert that was intentionally similar to a fire engine's siren.

"Sorry," Cyn said as she fumbled it out of her pocket. "That's the ringer I use for the firehouse."

"No kidding," Mari said, giving Cyn a smirk as she stepped back and answered the call.

"Robinson," she said, and it was a strange feeling switching back over to work mode in that circumstance. Ordinarily, the siren was what got her adrenaline flowing. But considering what she'd been doing just before, it was a let-down this time.

"We've got a three-alarm in progress," came James's voice. "I'm sorry, I know you're at that Grimm House thing, but we need you at the scene."

"Is it arson again?" she asked, catching the concerned look in Marigold's eyes as she listened to one half of Cyn's conversation.

"I don't know," James said. "Get here as quick as you can, okay? The first two trucks are leaving now and we need all hands on deck."

"Okay," Cyn said, ending the call and stuffing the phone back into her pocket. Then she looked regretfully at Marigold. Nothing short of a three-alarm fire could have pulled her away in that moment. "I'm sorry, I have to go."

"I heard," Mari said.

Cyn didn't want the moment to end – she was desperate to make it go on as long as she could, because she was still half-convinced she'd wake up in the morning to find that it was all a dream. All she could come up with was, "Do you want to walk me to my truck?"

"Sure," Marigold said. Cyn reached for her hand and they left the library.

"Thanks for showing me the library," Cyn said as they hurried toward the stairs. In the distance, she could hear the string quartet playing – something a little livelier now that everyone had finished their meals. "I have to confess, I was sort of hoping to dance with you properly in the ballroom. I could hold you in my arms all night."

Marigold blushed at the idea, then picked up the hem of her skirt as they headed down the stairs. "I'd like that, although honestly, it's probably better this way. It wouldn't make for a very good tribute to my father's work here if tomorrow morning the newspapers were splashed with pictures of the two of us. I'm not exactly *out*."

"Would your father disapprove?" Cyn asked with a frown.

"It's not that," Mari said. "He knows. But I've never made dating much of a priority, so I don't know how many other people know."

"I didn't," Cyn admitted. "Although I spent a lot of years hoping I wasn't imagining the sparks when we were kids."

"You weren't," Mari said as they got to the bottom of the stairs.

The foyer was empty for the moment, so Cyn decided to be bold. She cupped Marigold's face in her hands and pressed her up against the ornate bannister for another quick kiss. "Good."

They went outside, their hands still linked, and when Cyn noticed Mari wobbling as her heels sank into the gravel, she tucked her hand under her arm for support. They went over to her truck, conspicuous as one of the few non-luxury vehicles in the lot, and Cyn grabbed her backup boots out of the foot well. At least she'd come prepared.

While she slipped off her nice loafers and hurried into the old, grungy boots, Mari asked, "What made you want to be a firefighter?"

"I wanted to do something where I could help people," Cyn said. That was the typical answer she heard the guys at the firehouse giving whenever it came up, but as she said it, the words sounded cliché. They weren't false, but they weren't the whole story, either. As she bent to lace up her boots, she said, "Actually, it had a lot to do with my stepmother's boutique. She wanted me to work there after high school, and be this completely different person – feminine, demure, stylish. When my best friend, Gus, went to career day to sign up for the police academy, I went with him and the fire department's booth caught my eye."

She laughed as she stood up, keeping her attention on Marigold's entrancing face as she set her loafers in the truck.

Then she added, "It was the only rebellious teenage moment I ever had, and Samantha never forgave me for it. I'm not sure Drew did, either. He thought I was showing him up."

"Well, they're fools because I don't know what I would have done without your help this morning," Marigold said.

"I never imagined the day would end like this," Cyn answered. She really should have left by now, but what would one more kiss hurt? She wrapped her arms around Mari and just as their lips met, the grandfather clock in the foyer chimed softly in the distance. Cyn tore herself away and said, "I'm sorry, I have to go. Thank you for a wonderful evening."

Marigold stepped back and Cyn jogged around to the driver's side door, then drove off without a backwards look – she didn't think she'd have the courage to leave, fire or no fire, if she saw Marigold in her rearview mirror.

FOURTEEN
MARIGOLD

Marigold watched Cyn's truck fly out of the parking lot and turn the corner around the building. As the clock finished its twelve bells announcing the hour, Mari laughed to herself and put her fingers to her lips. Ever since Cyn pulled her into that very welcome kiss in the library, she felt like she was floating a few inches above the ground. She glanced down and that's when she noticed a single, carefully polished loafer laying in the gravel at her feet.

Cyn must have dropped it as she was changing into her boots and it made Marigold smile because it meant Cyn had been just as flustered about the whole evening as she was. Mari picked up the shoe and carried it back into the house, placing it in a woven basket beneath the console table in the foyer for safekeeping.

This just means I'll have to see her again, she though, and that was an idea she liked very much, even as she admitted to herself that the timing was terrible.

Her whole life, Marigold had never given much thought to her love life. She dated a little in college, but as soon as her feelings for someone started to interfere with her work at Grimm House, she had no problem cutting ties and getting back to work. Running this place was all she ever wanted and she didn't mind making sacrifices in the name of that goal.

Now, on the eve of her father's retirement, her head was dizzy with thoughts of Cyn's lips on hers.

Marigold stood in the hall outside the grand ballroom, carefully smoothing the tulle of her dress to erase any evidence of her library tryst. Marigold planned to have a wife and family someday, but now was the worst possible time to fall in love.

She stepped into the ballroom and her father called from across the room, "Ah, there's my beautiful princess."

He waved her over. He was standing with Emily and Ryan, as well as the mayor of Grimm Falls. Marigold's cheeks burned with a sudden swell of shame – how could she have taken time out of such an important event to make out with a woman who, for all intents and purposes, she'd just met this morning?

How could I not? the more carnal parts of her brain fired back.

Emily weaved her way through the crowd to retrieve Mari. She took her hand, then asked with a wry smile, "What happened to your gloves?"

Mari looked down at her bare hands, noticing their absence for the first time. They were probably still draped over the arm of her favorite leather chair in the library, where Cyn had left them after she slowly, sensuously peeled them from Marigold's hands.

"They were too difficult to eat with," Marigold fibbed. "I took them off."

"It wouldn't have anything to do with a certain attractive firefighter, would it?" Emily asked, leaning her head in close to talk confidentially to Mari. "I saw you two leave almost an hour ago."

"No, of course not," Marigold objected. She brushed down the tulle one more time just to be sure it was in place, then adjusted her wristwatch so the face was perfectly centered. "I was dealing with the caterers."

"Liar," Emily said, grinning. They were almost to Mari's father and the mayor, and she added quickly, "I think the two of you would be a good match. Don't shut her out."

Mari had to resist the urge to roll her eyes. They'd been working together so long, Emily thought she knew her better than Marigold knew herself. That included making attempts at mind-reading, which were particularly annoying when they were accurate.

"Hi, how's everyone doing?" Marigold asked as she approached the group, putting on her best, pearly smile.

"We were beginning to wonder if you were ever coming back," Ryan said as Mari reached out to shake the mayor's hand. He was an older gentleman with pure white hair, known for playing Santa Claus in the city's annual Christmas play.

Mari gave Ryan a toothy smile and said, "You know

how these big events go. Someone always needs something."

"Well, it's getting late," her father said. "I was just about to thank everyone for being here. Perhaps you'd like to sit at the mayor's table?"

Marigold shot a charming smile at the mayor and said, "It would be an honor."

He escorted her to a table near the front of the room with an excellent view of the podium, and pulled out her chair. She sat, and Ryan claimed the empty seat on the other side of the mayor. He sat ramrod straight and kept his eyes fixed on the podium, and Marigold adopted a similar posture.

Game on.

Emily and Marigold's father went to the front of the room. Emily took the podium first, moving the potted bluebell gently to the side to gain access to the microphone. She got everyone's attention and waited patiently for the room to settle down. People returned from the bar and the dance floor, taking their seats, and then Emily turned the microphone over to Marigold's dad. He buttoned his tuxedo jacket and stepped behind the podium, closing his large fists around the edge of the lectern and clearing his throat.

"I hope everyone has had a wonderful evening tonight," he said. "I want to thank each and every one of you for being here to celebrate the work I've done at Grimm House. I also want to give a special thanks to my lovely daughter, Marigold, for putting this whole event together. I know what a burden party planning can be."

He paused for a polite round of applause and a lot of eyes turned to Marigold sitting beside the mayor. She nodded and gave a modest wave, and it didn't escape her notice that Ryan's name was conspicuously absent from her father's thanks. He'd noticed how hard she worked, and how she'd done it all on her own.

"As you all know, I'm due to retire soon," her father went on. He grinned and said, "I am what you would call an old fart." Everyone laughed and he paused again to bask in his joke. Then his demeanor became serious and Marigold's heart began to beat a little faster. *This is it.* "My work here is nearly done, but Grimm House will continue to be a source of culture and history in our community. That's in no small part thanks to the generosity and support of everyone here, as well as my own brilliant daughter, Marigold. She works tirelessly on the many events that Grimm House hosts every year, and I am sure that as I prepare to step down, the services we provide will continue to be integral to the community thanks to Marigold's ingenuity."

A hot flash rippled through her body as she prepared for the moment she'd been craving over the last ten years. Would he call her up to the podium to stand beside him as he passed her the reins? She wondered briefly if she might pass out from the anticipation alone.

No, that is absolutely not on the table, she thought. *I am not going to pass out, I'm going to stand up and smile proudly because I deserve this moment.*

Her father opened his mouth to speak again, drawing a deep breath, and then he said, "We've got a delicious dessert planned, I believe it's a black forest cake from the Sweet Tooth Fairy bakery. Is that right, princess?"

Two hundred heads turned toward Marigold and she was working harder on maintaining her plastic smile than ever before as it dawned on her that her father was wrapping up his speech. Not a single word said about his retirement plans or the new management structure of the estate. All she could do was nod, so Ryan answered for her.

"That's right, black forest cake. I tasted it this morning and it's amazing."

Another ripple of laughter went through the room and then Mari's father ended his speech with a round of applause. Mari felt stuck to her chair. She didn't even clap – she was too stunned – and Ryan put his hand on her shoulder.

He didn't say anything - he didn't have to. Marigold wondered if he was going to wait until he got home to jump for joy, or excuse himself to the little boy's room and do it now.

Her father left the podium and the room began to stir with activity again. Some people headed back to the bar while others were aiming for her father to give him their congratulations personally. The army of waiters brought out dessert plates with the decadent black forest cake, and someone set one in front of Marigold, saying, "Here you go, miss."

"Thank you," she said, trying not to feel too heartbroken. She'd lost the battle for some reason she couldn't understand, but the war wasn't over. As she watched her father work the room, accepting accolades from all his past business associates and his friends, she picked up her fork and stabbed her piece of cake.

It was covered in a thick layer of whipped cream and sprinkled with dark chocolate shavings. She closed her eyes as she slipped the bite into her mouth and the chocolate melted against her tongue. It really was amazing, and not a half-bad salve for the disappointment she was feeling.

"Marigold Grimm?" she heard someone ask behind her chair when she was several bites deep in the rich cake.

She'd given up on decorum, indulging in the moment, and there was cake and whipped cream stuffed into her cheeks. All she managed was, "Hmm?"

She turned around and saw a man in the dress blues of a police officer. He asked, "May I join you?"

Marigold swallowed, then sat up straight and set down her fork. She pointed to the empty chair beside her and said, "Please."

"I'm not sure if we've met," the man said, extending his hand to her. "I'm Detective Steven Holt. I'm the fire investigator and I'm looking into the attack on your garden."

"Oh, good," Mari said, shaking his hand. "It's nice to meet you. Is there anything I can do to help, Detective?"

"Yes, actually," he said. He glanced down at the piece of cake on the table in front of him, left for the mayor, and asked, "Can I eat this?"

Mari reached across him and picked up the cake

someone had left in front of Ryan's chair, saying, "Here, this one's all yours."

"Thanks," Detective Holt said, picking up a fork. "Anyway, I read the statement you gave the firefighters this morning. It was very helpful, and I noticed that it said you saw the perpetrator. It would be very helpful if you could come down to the police station so we can create a police sketch based on what you saw."

"I'd be happy to," Marigold said, "but it was dark, and I only got a glimpse of him. I'm not sure how much help I'd be."

"Our sketch artists are very good at teasing out details," Detective Holt said, stuffing a large bite of Ryan's cake into his mouth. "Could you come to the station tomorrow and give it a try?"

"Of course," Marigold said. "I'm happy to be of assistance, and I want to thank you for looking into it."

"Just doing my job, miss," he said. He took another big bite, then held out his hand and said, "Thank you for your time, and for this lovely event."

He excused himself and Marigold went back to picking at her cake. She watched her father moving around the room, collecting congratulations on his as-yet undisclosed retirement. The sense of disappointment had been dulled a little by the sugar rushing through her veins, and by Detective Holt's visit. It brought her mind right back around to Cyn again, and the impossibility of taking the chemistry between them further while also trying to balance brand new duties at the estate.

Of course, that didn't mean she *wanted* to sit here in

uncertainty, wondering when and how her father would pass the torch.

The next time she had a chance to talk to her father was about an hour later, when the first of the guests had begun to trickle out and they formed a receiving line in the foyer to see them out. She stood with her father, thanking people for attending and wishing them a good night, and when they had a moment alone, he said, "I know you were looking forward to me announcing something about my retirement tonight, princess, but the timing wasn't right."

"I'm not trying to push you out," she said. "You can stay as long as you like. I was just hoping to hear something concrete."

"I'm still planning to retire, and soon," he said, trying to reassure her. "I'm just not sure now is the right time to be making those decisions."

Marigold knit her brow. Before tonight, it hadn't even occurred to her that this outcome was possible. The worst-case scenario had always been that she'd be saddled with Ryan.

"Why not?" she asked.

"I just want to make sure that we're making the right move for all involved," her father said. "I'll make my decision soon - you have my word on that. And I really did mean what I said in my speech – you did an incredible job with the party and you should feel proud of yourself for that. I know I do."

"Thank you," Marigold said.

She knew he was proud of her, but she also knew she

wouldn't be getting the restful sleep tonight that she had been craving – and her father's announcement, or lack thereof, wasn't the only reason.

As they stood in the foyer saying goodbye to their guests, her eyes kept going to the loafer sitting in the basket beneath the console table beside her.

FIFTEEN
LEVELING UP

The empty swimming pool turned out to be the best stroke of luck he'd had in a long time.

It was in the side yard of a house with a sad, beat up real estate sign in the front yard. All the grass was dead from years of neglect, choked with weeds and killed off from draught. The house itself looked just as ready to be torched as the barn had been, with pieces of its clapboard siding split and rotting, and a hole in the roof that seemed to grow bigger every time he looked at it.

He'd get around to doing that job eventually, satisfying the itch to bring another dangerous structure down. But not now. Not with a perfect vessel like that pool just lying around, begging him to use it.

The house was in the middle of nowhere, on another county road several miles outside the city, where people rarely ever went. This used to be farm country, but people had long since moved into the hustle and bustle of Grimm

Falls proper, and all the farmers had dried up just like their land.

He'd found this house one night when he couldn't sleep and he just started walking – a full pack of Winstons in his pocket, one tucked between his lips. His feet led him here, and when he caught sight of the pool, he knew it was on purpose.

As good as it felt to strike the wheel of his lighter, to hear the crackle of flames biting into wood, and to send a message to Grimm Falls, the truth was that what happened at Grimm House was a little too close for comfort.

Marigold Grimm had seen him. She was three stories up and it was dark so he couldn't say how well, but he ran out of there like his life depended on it, and then he spent the rest of the day waiting for someone from the police department to pound on his door.

He stuffed his favorite pair of work boots with the singed toes into the back of his closet. He thought about the alibi he'd give – he could say he picked up a late shift at work and no one would be the wiser. His boss never knew what half the guys were up to and as long as he filled out his time card to say he was working, then that was the truth. Then he thought about all the hasty mistakes he'd made in the garden, and imagined the questions the cops would have.

Marigold Grimm says she recognized you.

Is this your cigarette butt?

Are these your fingerprints on this gas can?

He should have wiped everything down, or at least

worn gloves. He should have been smarter, but the itch had been too great and he gave in to the urge when the opportunity presented itself. If he wanted to torch the garden before the old man's retirement, he had no choice but to work fast.

But no one ever came around and the more time he spent terrified of getting caught, jumping every time the elevator dinged in the hall outside his apartment, the more determined he was to avoid that panic in the future.

He still had a message to send, and he wanted to do that without ending up in the slammer. That meant taking it slow, planning his next moves, and being very deliberate in his actions. He already had his next target in mind, and he was beginning to think it should be his last. That was the lesson all those cop dramas taught you on TV – the longer you carried on and the cockier you got, the higher the chances were that you'd screw up somehow and end up in handcuffs.

It didn't sound like the police department was having any luck pinning the first two fires on Braden Fox, and that meant he had to be doubly careful not to leave any clues about his real identity.

That was why the pool was perfect - isolated, quiet, and contained.

He hated lugging those two heavy gas cans all the way to Grimm House, and the smell was nothing to write home about. The cans themselves were problematic, forcing him to either leave them at the scene or make an awkward escape with them thumping against his sides. He fully intended to learn from his mistakes, and the next fire was going to be his masterpiece.

That's why he came out here with a half-dozen empty beer bottles, an old t-shirt, a funnel, a single gallon of gasoline in a repurposed milk jug, and a cheap bottle of vodka.

He crouched in the deep end of the empty swimming pool and pulled all the ingredients for a set of Molotov cocktails out of the duffel bag he'd slung across his chest.

He'd looked up the directions that afternoon – on a public library computer terminal because he wasn't a blithering idiot. He put the funnel into the first bottle, filling it halfway with gasoline. He assembled the Molotov according to the instructions he'd found online, then stood up and took the lighter out of his pocket. He wasn't feeling particularly itchy now – just excited, with a nervous quiver in his stomach.

He flicked the lighter and touched the little orange flame to the damp tip of the rag. It ignited quickly, and when he felt the heat on his hand, he chucked the bottle toward the shallow end of the pool. It exploded in a spray of gasoline and glass that scattered across the concrete floor and created a puddle of fire.

It burned for a pleasingly long time, sending black plumes of smoke into the sky. When the flames finally went out, he bent down to prepare another one.

SIXTEEN
MARIGOLD

Mari hardly slept after the party was over, just like she predicted. It was well past midnight by the time the last guest left and she dismissed the staff, and then she lingered downstairs.

There was no reason to think that the arsonist would be back for a second attack, particularly if the first one had been motivated by her father's retirement party. But she couldn't shake the concern that he might come back to finish the job. It was easier to just stay awake, and there was more than enough clean-up to keep her busy, so she changed into a pair of jeans and a t-shirt and started tidying the ballroom.

Besides, she thought, *it would be a shame if Cyn came back for her missing shoe and I was asleep.*

She cleaned for a while, and kept an eye on the garden just in case. She sat down on the chaise lounge in the parlor at the back of the house around two a.m. to rest her feet for a few minutes, thinking fondly of the foot massage Cyn had given her. Her eyes grew heavy, and when she woke up four hours later, the house had begun to stir with activity again.

There were breakfast sounds coming from the professional-grade kitchen down the hall – pots and pans clattering and the hiss of a kettle coming to a boil. Just because the retirement party was over didn't mean Grimm House got to rest on its laurels for so much as a day, and there was a ladies' tea hour that happened in the garden every fourth Sunday morning.

Mari groaned and got out of the chair. Her clothes were wrinkled and her skin felt stiff from spending the whole night in the formal makeup she'd put on for the party.

She popped her head into the kitchen, where she found the estate's head chef bright eyed and bushy tailed, cleaning a bunch of spinach to make his famous mini quiches for the tea hour. "Federico, have you seen Emily yet this morning?"

"No, miss," he said. "She usually starts at seven, doesn't she?"

"What time is it?" Mari asked, and when he saw how tired she was, Federico pressed a warm mug of coffee into her hands.

"It's only six," he said. "When I see Emily, I'll tell her you're looking for her."

"Thank you," Mari said, taking a long, grateful sip from the coffee cup. It was hot and strong – *how I like my women*. The stray thought popped into her mind before she could chase it away, and she grinned at the fact that Cyn was who she pictured. She shook away the idea, then said, "I just need to talk to her about the tea party location – I was so wrapped up with the retirement party, I forgot that those ladies probably don't want to look at the pathetic remains of my garden during their tea time."

"I'll let her know," Federico said, turning back to his spinach.

Mari took another long sip of her coffee, then headed upstairs to take a shower and change into something more appropriate for a new day. It was amazing what even a few hours of sleep could do for a girl's perspective – the pity party over her father's delayed announcement had officially ended and Marigold was ready to take on another day at Grimm House.

❋

MARI CAME BACK DOWNSTAIRS an hour later, feeling refreshed and more like herself with a hot shower and a cup of coffee behind her. She found Emily and discovered that she'd already moved the ladies' tea hour to the terrace closer to the building. Not only that, but she'd spearheaded the removal and storage of all the tables and chairs in the ballroom, and everything was looking nearly back to normal.

"Good morning," Mari said, wrapping her arms around Emily for a quick hug. "Thank you for dealing with the tea hour. I barely slept last night."

"You're welcome," Emily said. "But are you that

concerned with your father's retirement? You know the estate will be yours."

"I was so sure he was going to make his official announcement last night," Marigold said. "I don't understand what changed his mind."

Emily cast her eyes away. Mari had been expecting sympathy and commiseration, and instead she was beginning to feel suspicious.

"What?" she asked. "Do you know something?"

"I may have *done* something," Emily said, looking sheepishly at Marigold. "I saw you in the garden with that firefighter."

"Cyn," Mari said, her heart sinking into her stomach. "What did you do, Em?"

"Don't kill me," Emily said. As if anyone who had ever prefaced a confession with that plea had lived to tell about it. "I really think your father has a point about how little time you'll have for a social life if you're running the estate all by yourself. I saw the way you were looking at that girl."

"What did you do?" Mari repeated.

"I told your father about her," Emily said. "If there's something between the two of you, I think it would be a shame to ignore the possibility. I thought if you just had a couple more weeks before a whole new set of responsibilities were dumped in your lap, you could really think about what you'll be sacrificing." Perhaps Emily saw the glint in Marigold's eye that said she dearly wanted to strangle her in that moment, because she added, "I meddle out of love."

Marigold pinched the bridge of her nose between her fingers, trying to process this turn of events. Then she asked with a sigh, "Where's Ryan?"

"In his office," Emily said. "I think he's working on the social calendar for next season. Do you need him?"

"No, let him work. I have some business to attend to downtown," Marigold said. She needed to see about having that police sketch done, and she also wasn't sure how long she could bear to look at the blackened, wilting flowers visible from every south-facing window in the house, so a trip to Green Thumb would be in order, too. "Can you hold down the fort?"

"Sure," Emily said. Mari turned to leave, and Em called after her, "Don't forget the loafer in the foyer." Marigold turned back to give her a quizzical look and Em just winked and said, "That's right, I saw it."

Mari rolled her eyes, but she grabbed the loafer out of the woven basket on her way out of the house. She went to the terrace first, checking on the setup for the tea hour and making sure it was all coming together. Then she ducked under the caution tape strung across her garden and went to the long, wide pathway where the damage was the worst.

Thirty-six hours after the fire, it looked even more decimated than before. The perpetrator had dumped ten gallons of gasoline on her poor flowers and plants. Everything the fire had touched was blackened, dried out and curling in on itself, and everything the gasoline had attacked was scarred, brown and wounded.

The waterlogged plants that had their leaves blown

off them might still make a comeback. The Cinderella milkweed that Mari had managed to rescue from the hoses was clinging to its delicate pink petals like its life hung in the balance, but if she didn't get it out of the tainted soil soon, it would all have to be replaced.

Marigold took out her phone and made a quick list of all the different types of plants she would need. She was always expanding the space, exploring exotic new plants and interesting configurations, but this stretch was a part of the original garden that her mother had planted over thirty years ago.

She was determined that when she was done rebuilding, it would look just like nothing had ever happened to it – with one exception. Marigold couldn't wait to find a place of honor for the bluebell that Cyn had given her last night.

Mari went into town and stopped at Green Thumb to give the nursery owner her wish list of plants, then she headed across the street to the police station to meet with the sketch artist.

❄

"WHAT ABOUT HIS NOSE?" the sketch artist asked.

Marigold put up her hands in frustration. She'd been answering *I don't know* and *I didn't get a good look at him* for the last twenty minutes, and she felt horribly unhelpful. She had no good answers and no matter how many options the sketch artist gave, she just didn't have that much to offer.

The sketch artist was persistent, though. "Would you say it was more aquiline? Button? Upturned? Wide or flat?"

"I don't know," Marigold said. "I'm sorry."

She was sitting in the small police station's break room, sipping water from a paper cup. The sketch artist had attempted to lead her into the interrogation room, explaining that it would be much quieter than sitting out there where phones could be heard ringing all over the office and people were walking back and forth to grab their lunches out of the fridge.

She didn't like that idea, though. Mari much preferred the bustle of people coming in and out of the break room rather than the steel table in the center of the interrogation room, with eyelets welded in the center of the table where cops could attach handcuffs for dangerous suspects. It was unsettling in an already uncomfortable situation.

"I really wish I could be more help," Mari told the sketch artist. "It's just that I was looking at him through a window, three stories up, and the only light was from the fire. He just looked like an average guy. He was an average height, wearing all black... just unremarkable."

"You're doing fine," the sketch artist said. "Trust me, Detective Holt understands that this is a long shot, but there's a process that I go through to make sure I get the most accurate sketch possible, even if we don't have many details to go on. You just never know what might be helpful."

He got up and went over to the water dispenser in the

corner to refill Marigold's cup and get one for himself. A couple more police officers came into the room to get their lunches out of the fridge, and then they sat down at an empty table at the other side of the room to eat.

The sketch artist sat down across from Marigold and picked up his sketchpad again, then asked, "What about his chin? Was it cleft? Square or pointy? Did he have facial hair?"

Marigold opened her mouth to speak, then closed it with a frown. She'd been about to say that his chin was just as unremarkable as the rest of him, but that wasn't right. There had been *something* remarkable about his chin.

She sat up a little taller, trying to remember. "There was something about his chin. I'm not sure what – a mole, a birthmark maybe, or a small amount of facial hair?"

"There, see?" the sketch artist asked, looking pleased with himself. "I told you details sometimes pop up when you least expect them. Now, how big would you say the mark was? Are we talking about covering most of his chin, or smaller than that?"

"Smaller, definitely," Marigold said.

The rest of the sketch took about five more minutes, and Marigold apologized when the image they'd produced wasn't a face she recognized.

"Is that unusual?" she asked. "Why would someone I don't even know torch my garden?"

"I'll make you some copies of the sketch," the artist said. "Maybe he's got a problem with your father or someone else at the house. Show the photo around and see if anyone recognizes him – maybe he came by the place recently to case it."

He left her in the break room momentarily to make copies of the sketch and Marigold glanced over at the officers who were quietly eating their lunch at the other table. They were young, in their early to mid-twenties like Mari, and talking about a case they'd just finished.

"I'm sorry to inconvenience you," she said. "I'm sure I'll be out of here soon."

"It's no trouble," one of them said. "We really shouldn't be talking shop at lunch anyway."

Then the sketch artist returned with a small stack of papers and handed them to her.

"If anyone recognizes him, have them call the station immediately," he instructed.

"Okay," Marigold said, folding the pages and tucking them into her purse. "Thank you so much, and thank Detective Holt for me. Everyone here, and at the firehouse, has been so kind. Especially Cyn Robinson – if it wasn't for her, I think my whole garden would be a lost cause right now."

"You know, the service awards are coming up in a couple of weeks," one of the policemen sitting at the other table said. "I'm sorry to nose into your conversation, but if you really want to thank Cyn, you could nominate her. The voting ends next week."

"That's a really good idea," Marigold said. "Thank you."

"My pleasure," the policeman said, and if she wasn't mistaken, he had a wry smile on his lips. Was he teasing her, or joking about the whole thing? But it was a good idea – Cyn deserved some recognition for what she'd done to preserve the garden.

"Is there a form to fill out?" Mari asked.

"Yeah," the young policeman said. "Just ask at the front desk."

"I will," Mari said.

She was halfway out of the break room when she heard the two guys cracking up behind her, the slightly older one saying, "Gus, you asshole – Cinders is going to kill you."

Mari smiled, then went to the front desk to ask for the form.

SEVENTEEN

CYN

"I hear you spent most of the party last night with a certain Miss Grimm," James said as Cyn came into the break room with a yawn and went to the coffee maker.

The fire last night turned out not to be another act of violence from the arsonist – this time, it was garden variety stupidity. A bunch of teenagers had been drinking and having fun and they started a bonfire a little too close to a field of dry brush. A little bit of alcohol, plenty of youthful naiveté and a heavy hand with the lighter fluid made for a pretty big brush fire.

By the time the blaze was extinguished, it was three a.m. and Cyn had a shift starting at seven. Instead of going all the way back to the carriage house on the other side of town, she changed into an oversized fire department t-shirt and a pair of sweats, then crashed in the bunk room upstairs, too tired to go home.

The guys let her sleep in a while since there was

nothing going on, and it was a little before noon when she came downstairs. Now, as she poured herself a cup of coffee, a satisfied smile spread across her lips at the thought of Marigold.

"I'll take that as a yes," James said. "Come on, you know we like details when we're bored around here."

Cyn looked at him, then at the other two members of her crew sitting at the break room table. Ordinarily, she'd shut down this type of teasing, or toss it right back at them. *What's it like to go home to the same woman every night for fifteen years?* she might have ribbed James, and had done so on many occasions before. But today, she was feeling sappy. Today, she was pretty sure the answer was, *It's incredible.*

"Did Frank tell you?" she asked.

James nodded. "He said you disappeared right after dinner and he saw you going upstairs with a certain prim and proper socialite."

Cyn smiled. "You know, she's really not as prim as she seems. She can get her hands dirty when she wants."

"Dirty, huh?" Gleeson said. "So, does that mean the rumors are true? Are my chances with her officially zero?"

Cyn laughed and said, "Your chances with Marigold Grimm have *always* been zero."

She sat down at the table and sipped her coffee, slowly adjusting to being awake. It was nice when she had that luxury – as much as she loved the thrill of the job, waking up to a siren blaring at full volume and a room full of firefighters scrambling to get dressed was not the most peaceful way to greet the day.

"I talked to the fire inspector a little bit last night," she said. "He doesn't like our Braden Fox theory. Apparently, the guy has an alibi for both the museum and the barn fire – no word yet on the Grimm House garden, but Fox doesn't have much of a connection to the estate so there's no motive."

"Cinders, you know arson cases are really hard to solve," James said. "Even if the perp wrote his name in gas and lit it on fire for us, we'd still have a hard time proving it beyond a shadow of a doubt. Fire's just too destructive."

"Holt's not giving up," Cyn said. "And neither am I."

"Okay, Sherlock Holmes," he said. "Now the more important question is, who's up for a quick game of poker before our next call?"

❄

CYN WAS WORKING ON A FLUSH, concentrating hard on the game, when one of the guys kicked her shoe under the table.

"What?" she asked, a little irritated, and when she looked up, Marigold was standing in the doorway.

She wore a flowing blouse with navy polka dots and little ruffles that accentuated her curves. Her long legs seemed to go on for days in a pair of matching, straight-legged slacks that hung over pointy-toed heels. Her dusty blonde hair hung in wavy locks over her shoulders, and in her right hand, there was a familiar black loafer.

Cyn was transfixed by the sight of her in the harsh fluorescents and somewhat dingy surroundings of the firehouse.

"Hi, Cyn," Mari said, and the way she looked at her, it was like there was no one else in the room. "I was in town, running a couple of errands, and I wanted to return your shoe. It must have fallen out of your truck when you left last night."

"Very slick," James said out of the corner of his mouth and Cyn gave him a sharp look.

Actually, it *would* have been slick if she'd had any clue that her shoe was missing. She hadn't had time to think about it, or the suit that she'd left hanging in the closet upstairs, or the gold chain that she'd stored in her glove compartment for safe-keeping until she could return it to its place in her jewelry box.

"Thank you," Cyn said, getting up. She set her cards face-down on the table instinctively, even though she'd lost all interest in the game the moment she saw Marigold. She joined Mari in the doorway and took the loafer from her, their fingers gliding over each other during the transfer and reawakening the spark that she'd felt last night in the library. "I would have been heartbroken if I thought I'd lost this."

Mari looked over Cyn's shoulder, to where a table full of firefighters were staring at the two of them, not even pretending otherwise. Then she said, "I hope it's okay that I came."

"You can come any time you like," Gleeson said and Cyn could have strangled him.

That was the price she paid for working in a male-dominated profession, and the reason why she would never choose to bring a woman she was interested in to the firehouse – not that it had ever come up before.

She ignored him instead, and Marigold did her the favor of doing the same. Cyn blocked his view with her back and said, "Thank you for bringing back my shoe. I'd ask if you're free for coffee, but I'm not really supposed to leave the firehouse while I'm on duty in case we get a call."

"That's okay," Mari said. "I understand."

Those blue eyes burned into Cyn and filled her whole body with electricity, and she felt like she was blowing her chance. She didn't want Marigold to walk out of the firehouse right now because they might never have an excuse to run into each other again.

"But we have coffee here," she blurted. "James buys the good stuff, actually – fair trade, organic. Would you like a cup?"

"Umm," Mari said, glancing at the other firefighters at the table, then back to Cyn. Her heart stopped in that moment of hesitation, then started up again with a leap of delight as Mari said, "I'd like that."

"That'll be five dollars a cup," James said as Cyn led Marigold over to the counter and got a fresh mug from the cabinet. "That's my toasted blackberry blend – very popular, very pricey."

"You can take it out of my chips," Cyn shot back,

nodding at the stack of poker chips in front of her unplayed cards. James shrugged and grabbed a couple chips off the top of the stack.

Cyn poured coffee into the mug and slid a little caddy full of cream and sugar packets across the counter to Marigold. She lifted the cup to her nose, taking in the aroma of fresh-brewed coffee and the faint notes of blackberry, and then in deference to James's high-brow coffee tastes, she sipped it black and gave him an appreciative smile.

"It's very good," she said. She took another sip and Cyn enjoyed the sight of her lips wrapping around the ceramic rim. She enjoyed it even more when Marigold's tongue slipped out and licked the liquid from her bottom lip.

"There's not much room down here to sit," Cyn said apologetically to Marigold. "Unless you want to hang out with these guys, or sit in a fire engine. But we could go up to the bunk room where it's a little quieter."

Her cheeks burned as she suggested it. They would be all alone up there and while that thought had certainly crossed her mind, she was more interested in getting away from the rest of her crew before they could embarrass her or make another crude joke.

"Well, the fire engine is tempting," Marigold said. "But I'll settle for the bunk room."

As Cyn led Mari out of the break room, the look James gave her was unmistakable. *Cinders and Marigold, sitting in a tree...*

She brought Mari over to a steel door just outside the break room and opened it to reveal a flight of stairs leading up to the living quarters where all the firefighters slept when they were on call. As she followed Mari into the stairwell, enjoying the view, she said, "I'm sorry about the guys – they get bored and antsy when there's nothing to do, and it can feel like being in a locker room sometimes."

"Don't worry," Marigold said, turning around and forcing Cyn to bring her eyes abruptly upward to avoid being caught in the very behavior she'd just distanced herself from. She noticed Cyn's gaze despite her best efforts, and gave her a toothy grin as she said, "I can hold my own."

"I never doubted you," Cyn said. Mari turned back around, her hand gliding up the railing, the curves of her ass and hips irresistible in her tight pants. Cyn smiled and said, "If you want, we'll take the fire pole when we come back down."

"You actually have one of those?" Marigold asked.

"Of course," Cyn said. "What self-respecting firefighter takes the stairs? You might want to lose the heels, though."

"You'd be amazed what I can do in these heels," Mari said as she reached the top of the stairs and turned around to face Cyn. There it was – that flirtation again. It had felt so surreal the night before, like something out of a dream or a fairy tale, but in the light of day, Cyn couldn't deny it.

She stepped forward, ready to kiss Marigold again,

but instead, Mari raised her coffee cup and took another sip, then turned and looked around the room.

"So, this is where you spend your time?"

"When I'm on call, yes," Cyn said. "Want the tour?"

"Please."

There wasn't too much to show her. The bunk room was one big space, with three sets of bunk beds pushed up against the walls on two sides, a couple of couches and a television set in the opposite corner, partitioned off by a rather ineffective room divider.

In the fourth corner, there was the fire pole. Cyn led Mari over to it and put one hand on the cool metal, circling slowly around the hole in the floor and keeping a professional distance between them. Mari peeked down to the first floor, then closed her eyes and leaned back.

"Afraid of heights?" Cyn asked.

"No," Marigold said. "I am afraid of falling, though."

Cyn got brave. She swung around the pole to meet Marigold, their bodies nearly touching as she said in her most sultry voice, "Don't worry. I won't let you fall."

Marigold bit her lower lip and Cyn could feel it between her legs, desire blooming hot and urgent. She leaned in again for a kiss, but again, Marigold pulled back. She smiled at Cyn and said, "So, you came into my world last night. Tell me about yours. What's it like being a firefighter?"

"It's pretty great," Cyn said. She took Mari's hand and led her over to the couches, where they sat down together and Marigold let Cyn's knee rest against hers. "There's a lot more sitting around, waiting, than I expected when I first started, but it didn't take long to figure out that's a good thing. The better I get at poker, the safer Grimm Falls is. But when we do get a call, oh, nothing beats the course of adrenaline that shoots through my veins at the sound of the alarm."

Mari smiled, amused. "So, you're an adrenaline junkie?"

"Not at first," Cyn said. "It used to scare me. But it grew on me, and it beats the hell out of the alternative – working in my stepmother's boutique and helping stuffy rich ladies try on overpriced clothes that will probably never leave their walk-in closets." She glanced at Marigold. The heels she wore today had those red soles that told Cyn they probably cost what she made in a week, and nothing else Mari wore looked cheap, either. "Sorry – not that there's anything wrong with it."

Marigold laughed, then said, "It's okay. Would it make me sound more or less like a rich snob if I told you I leave all my clothes shopping to my assistant because she actually enjoys it?"

Cyn put her hand to her chin, thinking about it for a minute, then she said, "Less, as long as she's enjoying herself. How did the party go, by the way? Am I looking at the proud new conservator of Grimm House?"

Mari frowned for the first time since she'd arrived in the firehouse. "Not exactly. I was hoping my father would make an official announcement last night, but he had a change of heart and decided to wait a little longer."

"Oh, I'm sorry," Cyn said.

"It's okay," Mari said. "It's just a matter of patience at

this point. I love my father dearly but things have to feel just right for him to make a decision, and that goes double for any matters involving me. I'm sure you know, being an only child *and* having only one parent means the doting often borders on overbearing."

"Actually," Cyn said, "my dad took the opposite approach. My mother's death was hard on him, and when we moved to Grimm Falls, he was trying to circumvent the grieving process by throwing himself into his new marriage. He tried to do the same thing for me by throwing me into work at Samantha's boutique, but that didn't end well."

She said this last part with a roll of her eyes and Mari asked, "What happened?"

"You know, that timeless story – surly tomboy with a dead mom meets ultra-feminine stepmother, proves incapable of fitting into the boutique's image and winds up causing resentment all around," Cyn said with a shrug. She set her coffee mug on a nearby end table and added, "We both tried to make it work for my father's sake for a while. I wore dresses and put on the expensive makeup Samantha bought me. I kept trying to be the girly girl she wanted, but sooner or later, it always fell apart. It's impossible to be who two different people want you to be, even when one of those people is you."

"Well, I like the real version of you," Marigold said, and then she abruptly leaned in for the kiss Cyn had been waiting for.

EIGHTEEN
MARIGOLD

The kiss was impulsive.

Mari had been trying to resist the urge to act on her desires ever since she came upstairs with Cyn – a bad idea that led her right into temptation. She shouldn't have been sending mixed signals like this to Cyn when she didn't know what she wanted or what kind of relationship she was capable of. Her future lay in her father's hands and until he made a decision, she couldn't make any for herself.

But sitting just a few inches away from Cyn, with those steely eyes boring into her, setting her core on fire, she couldn't help herself.

Cyn slid her tongue along Mari's lips, tickling them until they parted, and then her tongue was inside Marigold's mouth. The wetness, the firmness of the tip of her tongue as it danced over Mari's made her forget every hesitation she had except for one.

She pulled back and glanced toward the door to the stairwell. "Will we be interrupted?"

"No," Cyn said, planting her hands on the couch cushion on either side of Mari's hips and leaning into her space. "They may act like teenagers, but they're good guys. They won't pry."

Then she leaned further forward and Marigold felt her back pressing against the arm of the sofa. Her coffee cup was still in her hand and she reached awkwardly for the end table behind her head. Then Cyn took the mug from her and set it down, planting her lips on the tender skin of Marigold's collarbone in the same slick motion.

Mari let out a pleased moan and sank into the couch. She put her hands on Cyn's waist, feeling the core strength that she was engaging to hover above her. Then Mari pulled her down, spreading her legs so their hips connected.

They kissed and Cyn moved her hips against Marigold's body, gently at first, as if she was afraid of being caught in her desire and rejected. Meanwhile, Marigold ran her hands over Cyn's hips and down her backside, pulling her body closer as their tongues slid over each other.

The next time Marigold pulled back, it was because a sudden burst of fear bubbled up inside her and made her question what she was doing. She put her hand flat against Cyn's chest, pushing against her until she got the idea and pulled back. Mari said, "I'm sorry."

"Is something wrong?" Cyn asked. She sat up and

looked worried. "We are going kind of fast. We can just talk."

"I'd like that," Mari said. "But will you stay here on the couch with me?"

"Of course," Cyn said. Mari reached for her and Cyn lay down next to her, her arms wrapped around Marigold's waist and her head resting on her shoulder.

"I was being honest when I said last night that I don't normally do this sort of thing," Mari said. "I don't know how people do the whole one-night stand thing-"

"Is that what this is?" Cyn asked.

"No," Marigold hurried to add. "At least, I hope not."

"Good," Cyn said. "Besides, it would technically have to be a two-night stand."

"What I meant was," Mari said, then she paused to collect her thoughts and kiss the top of Cyn's head. Her hair was soft and fine, and it smelled like teakwood. "I've worked so hard on my career for the last ten years that I've never really had a personal life."

"So, what you're saying is that if you and I were to walk arm-in-arm down the streets of Grimm Falls, the paparazzi would have a field day," Cyn said.

"I don't have paparazzi," Mari said with a roll of her eyes. "But there probably would be talk. You know how everyone loves other people's business."

Cyn sat up so she could look Mari in the eyes, and she grabbed her hands to pull her upright. Then she asked, "So you've never had a girlfriend?"

"Not a serious one."

Then it was Mari's turn to be aggressive. She wanted

to escape this embarrassing admission so she grabbed Cyn's hand and yanked her back down on top of her, then threaded her fingers through Cyn's hair. She took Cyn's hand and put it on her chest, just above her heart so she could feel how hard it was beating. They looked into each other's eyes and she wished for a device that could stop time right in that moment.

Then Cyn slid her hand down a few inches to cup Marigold's breast. Her nipple hardened against Cyn's palm and her thumb moved in slow circles over the thin fabric of her blouse.

"I don't know how much of myself I could give you right now," Mari hurried to add before her desire could get the best of her. "If my father gives me control of the estate, I'll be really busy-"

"It's okay," Cyn said. "We can go as slow or as fast as you want. I'm not expecting anything. I just want to see where this goes."

"Okay," Mari said, giving in to Cyn's powerful seduction.

They kissed again and Cyn slid her hand over to Marigold's other breast, her thumb running over the most sensitive part and sending a deeper, more urgent wave of desire between her thighs. Then Marigold felt Cyn's hands sliding inside the V-neck cut of her blouse.

Her hands were warm and slightly rough from her work. Marigold gasped at the surge of pleasure as Cyn pulled her breast out of Mari's shirt and bowed to take her nipple into her mouth. She closed her eyes and arched her back, pressing her body against Cyn and closing her fist in her short hair.

She held Cyn's mouth against her as her tongue swirled wet and hot around her nipple.

Mari moaned, trying to stifle the sound and coming up short on willpower. Then Cyn's hips locked against Marigold's as her hand trailed over her waist and the curve of her hip bone. When their bodies moved together, Cyn's breath caught, sounding ragged in Mari's ear and driving her wild with desire.

She brought her hips closer and Cyn slid her hand around Mari's backside, then between her legs. She was hot and wet for Cyn and she could hardly keep her eyes open or her mind focused as everything became very small and far away, the whole world insignificant but for the curve of Cyn's body pressed against hers as her hand slid between Mari's legs.

She ran her fingers up and down over Marigold, then slipped her hand under the waistband of her pants. She parted her lips through her panties, and Mari nearly lost control when one finger slid inside of her. Mari let out a long sigh and Cyn shifted on the couch, laying Marigold down and straddling her. She put one hand over her mouth and whispered, "Sound travels up here. You have to be quiet."

Then she took her other hand from between Marigold's thighs and gave her fingers a lick, not breaking Marigold's gaze. She kissed her, their hips grinding together as Marigold delighted in the way their bodies moved together.

Cyn was wearing a pair of lightweight sweatpants and her navy fire department t-shirt, and she managed to look damn sexy in sweats. Marigold slipped her hands beneath the shirt hem to find Cyn's small, bare breasts. Her nipples were hard and she closed her eyes, trying hard to take her own advice as Marigold's hands closed over her breasts.

Be quiet. Be quiet.

As the desire built with every gyration of their hips, Mari wondered how much longer she could stay quiet. Cyn seemed to read the tortured look on her face, so she trailed one finger over Marigold's lips and then scooted down to the bottom of the couch. She unbuttoned Mari's pants and scrunched them down around her hips until they were at her ankles and her knees fell open.

Cyn slid her fingers over the fabric of Marigold's panties again, the smile on her face telling Mari that she was enjoying the tease of making her wait. Then she hooked the crotch of her panties aside and Marigold drew in an expectant breath. *Is this really happening?*

Cyn touched her gently at first, their eyes locked. She ran her fingers all over Marigold, spreading her wetness around. When she wet her clit, Marigold immediately let out a moan and clamped her hand over her mouth as Cyn lingered there, rolling her finger in slow, deliberate circles. Marigold closed her knees against Cyn's sides, squeezing her as Cyn slid a finger inside her again.

When Marigold began to rock her hips in time with Cyn's touch, she increased the intensity of her strokes and even though Mari wanted that moment to last forever, it wasn't long before she was crying into the palm of her hand, muffling the sounds of her orgasm.

As soon as she came, she reached up and pulled Cyn by her neck to lay down beside her again on the couch cushions. Their bodies pressed together closely in the narrow space and she kissed Cyn as she slid her hand down the front of her sweatpants. She was already throbbing with the first promise of release and Marigold ached to give it to her.

She didn't get it, though, because the moment Marigold felt the firm, wet mound of Cyn's clit, a siren started to blare from a speaker mounted to the wall nearby.

Mari sat up, her heart slamming into her chest. "What is that?"

"Shit," Cyn said, holding Marigold's hand against her for a moment longer. "That's the fire alarm. I have to go."

Of course, it was. What else?

Mari looked down at Cyn, still moving her hips needfully against her hand. As soon as they got up from that couch, the real world would come crashing back in on them.

But Cyn was too much of a professional to ignore the call of duty. She pulled Marigold's hand out of the waistband of her sweats and kissed her fingertips, then stood up and held out her hand. "Come on, it looks like you get to try out the fire pole after all."

Marigold took her hand and stood up, straightening her clothes. Cyn pulled her into the most indulgent kiss she could afford in the brief time they had, pressing her hips longingly against Marigold's body. Then she went over to an armoire anchored to the wall and changed quickly into her firefighter's uniform. It happened in a flash but Mari enjoyed the view while it lasted, the lines of Cyn's thigh muscles visible as she shimmied out of the sweats and pulled on her pants.

Then she led Mari over to the fire pole and they glanced through the hole. The rest of the crew was moving about below them, getting ready to board a bright red fire engine. James noticed them and shouted up, "Come on, it's a house fire. We have to get going."

"Do you think it's the arsonist?" Marigold asked.

"I don't know," Cyn said. "It doesn't seem like his MO, but we don't know that much about him yet."

"Oh, that reminds me!" Marigold said. "One of my errands this afternoon was having a police sketch done of the man I saw in my garden. I didn't see much, but they said it might help anyway. You should take a copy."

She dug into her purse and pulled one of the carefully folded copies the sketch artist had given her of his rendering. She smiled as she slid it into the pocket of Cyn's jacket.

"Thanks. I'll take a look on the way over," Cyn said.

Below them, James shouted, "Cinders, what are you waiting for, a formal invitation?"

She looked down through the hole in the floor again – something that probably didn't even faze Cyn anymore, but which made Marigold's knees lock up. When Cyn noticed her biting her lip, she said, "I have to get down there, but you can take the stairs if you want."

"No way," Mari said. She was not about to leave Cyn with the impression of her standing there like a chicken in her expensive, impractical heels. She grabbed the metal pole and Cyn told her how to wrap her legs around it to control her descent. Then she took a deep breath and did it, feeling weightless as she glided to the bottom with a big smile on her face.

NINETEEN
CYN

Cyn knocked on the door to her stepbrother's apartment and when he didn't answer, she switched to pounding on it.

"Drew, it's me. We need to talk," she said. She was biting back her anger as hard as she could and she included everything except the *or else*, but he still made her wait two more long minutes before he finally opened the door.

"What?" he asked as he yanked it open and gave her one of his signature annoyed looks. He was wearing his security uniform, a khaki work shirt and black pants, although the utility belt was missing. It was a little past five o'clock and Cyn had come as soon as she could after her shift ended.

It was all she could do to wait after she'd seen the police sketch Marigold had given her. Her heart stopped the moment she saw the face that looked back at her, and it was scowling at her right now.

She and Drew had never made good siblings – that was no secret. Cyn always hoped it had something to do with their three-year age difference, and that he would learn to appreciate her when they were older. If she'd held her breath hoping for that, she'd be dead a long time ago instead of standing in his doorway now with the police sketch tucked into her shirt pocket.

"We need to talk," she repeated. "Can I come in?"

She was doing her best to maintain an air of calmness. A large part of her was dying for Drew to come up with a believable reason why the sketch looked like him but wasn't him, why his alibis were airtight. Cyn had done a little digging into that this afternoon, quietly asking Gus to get the work logs for the security company where Drew worked and begging him not to ask questions yet.

Drew was on the clock during all three fires, but he'd punched himself in and out, and it was all overtime hours – nothing that involved being seen by anyone else in the company. And of course, he was working security at the museum during the first fire, so that didn't help his case.

Cyn's stomach was churning the whole way over to his apartment and she wanted to give Drew the benefit of the doubt, but there wasn't much doubt left on the table by now.

"I was just leaving, actually," Drew said.

"This won't take long," Cyn said. She nodded to his security uniform and asked, "Are you on your way to work?"

"No, just finished a shift," he answered. He was

blocking the door to his apartment with his body, standing tall and making Cyn's heart flutter in her chest. He was at least ten inches taller than her, and more than a hundred pounds heavier. He'd only ever been surly toward her, never violent, but if she was right about this... who knew what he'd do?

It was stupid to come here alone. She should have at least brought Gus with her for backup, but he was a cop. If she was right about her suspicions, Gus would be forced to act. She was here because she was hoping to resolve all of this without causing even deeper rifts in her already broken family.

She steeled her nerves and pulled the folded piece of paper out of her breast pocket. She opened it and turned it around for Drew to see. It wasn't a perfect match - the nose was a little too bulbous and the forehead was too high. Marigold had only seen him for a few seconds from a third story window, so that was to be expected. The patch of hair on his chin, though – that was harder to deny.

Then she said, "I don't want to talk about this in the hallway."

"What the hell is that?" he asked.

"A police sketch."

The smugness fell from his face. He snatched the paper out of Cyn's hand, then stepped reluctantly aside. "Fine. Come in."

Cyn stepped into the apartment. She'd only been here once or twice before, although Drew had lived here for the past five years. She'd never been inside, and she was surprised at how dark and messy the apartment was. The utility belt for Drew's work uniform lay on a table just inside the door, along with a lighter and a pack of cigarettes.

Winstons – the same brand they found in Marigold's garden, Cyn thought with a wave of nausea.

The other thing that hit her was the smell. Gasoline. It was faint, probably something that most people wouldn't even notice, but it was Cyn's job to recognize smells like that. When you ran into a burning building, certain accelerants burned off quickly and a firefighter who could say whether they smelled gas could be the difference between an arson conviction and an accidental fire.

Drew lived on the fourth floor of his apartment building and there was no reason for him to store gas there.

He glanced at the police sketch, then tossed it on the table near the door. "Is that supposed to be me?"

Cyn retrieved the sketch, folding it and putting it back in her pocket. "That's the man Marigold Grimm saw in her garden on the night of the fire. Where were you that night?"

She tried to make it sound like a casual question, the way police interrogators did on TV, but she was feeling anything but casual. By the way Drew was pacing in front of her, she guessed he felt the same.

"Working," he said. "At a concert on the other side of town. You can check the security logs."

"Is there anyone who can tell the police they actually saw you there?" Cyn asked.

"What the hell is all this?" Drew snapped. "If you've got something to say, just say it."

"Okay," Cyn said. "When did you start smoking again?"

She picked up the lighter on the table and Drew came over and snatched it out of her hand. "Don't touch that. Don't touch anything."

"I know you don't like Anthony Rosen," Cyn said. "You think he's making more of his life than you have, even though you're older. And you were there when the painting was set on fire. The barn... well, half the kids who have grown up in Grimm Falls have connections to that barn, but you and I both know you have a reason for wanting to burn it down. Why the Grimm House garden, though? I can't figure out the connection there."

"You're way off base, sis," Drew said with a sneer. "I didn't set any fires."

"Don't lie to me. I already know the truth," Cyn said. She'd come to the apartment ready to bluff – it was nice to know that all that time spent playing poker at the firehouse was good for *something* – but when she saw the cigarettes and smelled the gasoline, that was all the evidence she needed. "You're lucky they haven't caught you already, you know. You've been careless."

She picked up the pack of cigarettes and tossed them at Drew. They hit his chest and he caught them.

"We found your cigarette butt," she said. "And you

can't deny that sketch is a pretty close match. Why would you do it, Drew?"

Drew's expression shifted back into annoyance. "Do you really have to ask?"

"Yes," Cyn said. "Tell me, and maybe we can figure out a way to get you out of this."

The idea of letting a serial arsonist – and one who had done such atrocious damage to something with such immense sentimental value as Marigold's garden – made Cyn feel sick, but as much as she disliked him, Drew was family. The words tasted bitter in her mouth, but if he would let her help him, maybe the fires would stop and they could just put the whole ugly thing behind them.

He rolled his eyes at her.

"You're so fucking clueless," he spat. "You really think I would accept *your* help? After you stole everything from me?"

"What did I steal?" Cyn asked, her mouth dropping open.

"My mother!" Drew shouted. "You came here and took my entire life away from me. You took all of my mother's attention and you didn't even want it – it was like you were throwing it in my face every step of the way."

"I didn't ask for it," Cyn tried to object, but Drew was on a roll.

"Everything was about you, the daughter my mother always wanted," he said. "And when we grew up, it wasn't enough for you. You had to go be a heroic firefighter right after they turned me away from the police department."

"You flunked out of the academy," Cyn pointed out. She knew it wasn't the right time to be salting Drew's wounds, but she wasn't about to let him lay every bad thing in his life at her feet.

"You even managed to take Marigold," he said. "I had a crush on her since kindergarten, and who was the very first person you cozied up to when you get to Grimm Falls? Her."

Cyn felt her legs going to jelly. She stayed upright through sheer force of will as she asked, "You mean the reason you torched her garden was because of me? For what, revenge because of something that happened when we were kids?"

"Look how well that worked out," he said. "I heard about the retirement party. I guess that means you're fucking her now? Cynthia wins again."

"Don't talk about her like that," Cyn snapped. She had to bite back the urge to march across the room and slap him. "Why now? Didn't you already get payback for that a long time ago? I was still grieving my mother and having a friend could have made such a big difference in my life – whether it was you or Marigold. Instead, you made my life hell all through school."

"You made *my* life hell," Drew snapped. "And if you think she's into you now, you're dreaming. She's got her pick of anyone in this city – man or woman, if that's what she wants. Why would she choose you?"

Cyn pressed her lips together and closed her hands

into fists. She was fighting back the tears that Drew had so often conjured when they were younger. She knew this was nothing more than emotional manipulation, but his words cut straight to the insecurities deep in her core and she hated him for his ability to get to them so swiftly.

"Look, I have things to do tonight and I don't appreciate you coming over here to accuse me of crimes I didn't commit," he said. "Are we done here?"

"What are you going to do?" Cyn asked. "Set another fire?"

"That would imply I've set a fire in the first place," he said, sounding bored all of a sudden. He walked over to the door, dropping the pack of Winstons on the table as he went. Then he opened the door, sending Cyn a clear message. *Get out.*

There was nothing else she could accomplish here – not now. So she headed for the door, pausing before she got to the hall. She stood in Drew's personal space, their chests just a few inches apart as she did her best to rise to his nearly six-foot height.

"I came over here to warn you," she said. "It's the only one you're going to get. This town means too much to me, and Marigold Grimm means too much to me."

"Who deputized you?" Drew asked with a snort, dismissing her words. Then he pushed her shoulder, knocking her off balance as she stumbled into the hall and he closed the door.

TWENTY
SIBLING WARFARE

Drew was still in a sour mood several days after his evil stepsister showed up unannounced to threaten him and rub her perfect life in his face.

He'd curbed his desire to react in fiery, destructive ways. He'd even stopped himself from going back to the old, drained swimming pool despite the tremendous pleasure throwing Molotov cocktails gave him. It was too dangerous, and deprived of his new favorite form of stress release, he'd been grumpy. He kept the lighter in his pocket, rubbing his thumb over the soothing, smooth metal wheel all day long. He was doing just that, and worrying over what Cyn said to him, when he showed up to his weekly meal with his mother.

She doesn't know anything. She can't prove it or she would have gone to the cops already. She's just trying to do what she always does, and steal any little bit of joy out of my life.

Let her try.

He found his mother sitting at an outdoor table on the patio outside the restaurant. She was beautiful as always in a wide-brimmed hat that shaded the sun from her eyes, and she smiled warmly at Drew as he walked up the concrete path.

Cyn was nowhere to be found. Maybe she feels ashamed of what she said. Maybe she won't show her face around us anymore.

Drew's stepfather was sitting in his usual spot beside his mother, but that was okay. With one Robinson out of his hair, Drew could deal with the other one – Elliot hardly ever talked, anyway.

"Hi, angel," Drew's mother said as he leaned down to hug her and she put one bejeweled arm lightly around him. As he slid into the chair across from her, she exclaimed, "You shaved your chin."

Drew put his fingertips self-consciously to the newly bare skin where his soul patch had been. There was knowing that your evil stepsister was making idle threats, and then there was doing nothing to protect yourself. He wasn't stupid, and he knew he had to do something to distance himself from that police sketch the moment he saw it.

"I've had it since high school," he said, a little wistfully. "It was time for something new."

"Good. I always hated that thing," his mother said, laughing and taking a long sip of the margarita in front of her. She waved the waiter over for a refill and ordered one for Drew, too, then asked, "How was your week, angel?"

"Terrible," Drew said, not caring how much petulance

crept into his tone. He'd been waiting several days to complain about this to his mother, and he was going to enjoy it. "Cynthia paid me a visit at the end of the week. I thought she was finally coming around to the idea of us being brother and sister. I figured she wanted to hang out, like normal siblings do. Instead, I'm sure the whole reason she came over was to tell me that she's got a girlfriend or something, and remind me that she's doing better than me."

"That doesn't sound like my Cinders," *Elliot said, but when Drew shot him a piercing look, he averted his eyes to the table.*

Shut up, old man. You don't belong in this conversation, or this family, *Drew thought.*

"She said everything that's bad in my life is my fault," *Drew said.* "I don't know how she could say something so hurtful when she knows how badly I wanted to work for the police. The academy strung me along with false hopes and then hung me out to dry, and now she's reveling in it."

"You know how she likes to provoke people," *his mother said as she reached across the table and put her hand on top of Drew's. He didn't know where his dear stepsister was, but he was having an awful lot of fun lampooning her.*

"You know I'm doing the best I can, right, Mom?" *he asked.*

"Of course, angel," *she said, patting his hand. Then she glanced over his shoulder and said through clenched teeth,* "Here she comes."

Shit.

Drew turned around in his chair and couldn't believe his eyes as he saw Cyn marching up the path toward them. He'd been sure she would skip this and every family meal for some time to come after she'd had the nerve to stand there in his own apartment and accuse him of committing arson.

His mother gave Cyn a dirty look as she sat down in the fourth chair at their table, and that was worth every crocodile tear in the world. He wished he'd filmed it so he could play it over and over again on a loop.

"Where have you been?" his mother asked sharply.

Cyn glanced at Drew, giving him a look he couldn't quite read. Discomfort and maybe shame? That would be nice. Then she said, "I was at Grimm House, helping Marigold plant some bluebells in her garden."

"Does the fire department do landscaping now?" Drew asked, chuckling to himself and earning a smile from his mother.

Cyn shot back, "We do when someone defaces a community landmark."

"Cynthia," Drew's mom snapped. "We're at a nice restaurant and I'm sure I'm not the only one here who would appreciate it if you kept a civil tongue."

"Drew was the one who-" Cyn started to say, but his mother cut her off.

"It doesn't matter," she said with a deep roll of her eyes. "Honestly, it's like you're both still children."

Drew furrowed his brow. This was not going in the direction he wanted and he felt his blood beginning to boil. No matter what the situation, Cyn always found a way to worm out of it and put all the blame on him. He sneered as he said, "You always take her side."

"For heaven's sake, I'm not taking sides," his mother said, clearly exasperated with the subject. "If you want your stepsister to stop making you feel bad about your life, then do something to change it. I didn't raise you to walk around with your hand out, asking for other people to do all the hard work so you can reap the rewards."

Drew just sat there with his mouth open as the waiter returned with his margarita and a refill for his mother. He'd hardly gotten his wits about him before she turned her irritation on Cyn.

"And you," she said. "You can sit there and look innocent all you want, but we all know you're a pot stirrer. I knew it as far back as your teenage years. I go out of town on a business trip and what's the first thing she does? Abduct her father."

Drew sat back in his chair with a satisfied smile. He was hoping to get more sympathy from his mother after his little run-in with Cyn, but if she was going to jump straight to the infamous cemetery incident, this was okay too.

Cyn sat back, her arms crossed defensively over her chest, and said, "I didn't abduct him."

"Then why did he come back to Grimm Falls in a taxi?" Drew challenged her.

As much as he hated sharing memories with Cyn and her father, this was one of his favorite family stories. Cyn was sixteen and Drew was just out of high school. She'd just gotten her driver's license and his mother rewarded her with a ridiculous, pink Volkswagen Beetle. It wasn't the most expensive car in the world, and it was cheaper than the shiny, fully loaded Lexus that Drew had insisted on for his *sixteenth birthday – and then proceeded to wrap around a telephone pole a few years later. Easy come, easy go.*

But much to Drew's annoyance, Cyn loved that pink car. The color was no accident – it was intentionally chosen to force the femininity on her that Drew's mother wanted to see, but Cyn managed to look past it.

That's what made this story so delicious.

The very first time Drew's mother went out of town after she bought Cyn that car, Cyn dragged her dad with her to trudge up old memories and visit her mother's grave in Lisbon. He didn't want to go, but she refused to turn the car back around. When she stopped for gas, her dad called a taxi, and when Cyn finally came home late that night, Drew's mother was waiting up for her, ready to take away her keys.

She never saw that pink Beetle again, and Drew didn't stop smiling for a week.

Cyn wasn't smiling now, and that's how he liked it. Why should she smile after what she said to him last week? She had a lot of nerve threatening him like that, and he knew she didn't have anything on him.

She looked slightly tearful as she said, "That's not how I remember it."

TWENTY-ONE

CYN

You forget a lot of details in five years – more than you think you will.

By the time Cyn's sixteenth birthday rolled around, she couldn't remember the exact sound of her mother's laugh. She knew it was beautiful, but no matter how hard she tried or how many times she closed her eyes and tried to trigger the memory, it wouldn't come back. She knew her father was forgetting these details too, but whenever Cyn asked him, he didn't want to talk about her mother.

"It's not fair to Samantha," he would always say. "How would she feel if she knew I was waxing nostalgic about my previous wife?"

"I'm sure she thinks about her own late husband," Cyn mentioned once, but it did no good. Her father was a stone wall when it came to her mother, and Cyn knew he was protecting his own heart. He loved her too much to think about her, but Cyn loved her mother too much to forget.

Maybe it was selfish of her to try to take her father on that road trip. She had been dreaming of the day when she could go home to put flowers on her mother's grave, and just be near her again. When Samantha gave her that pink VW Beetle, Cyn had all the pieces – everything but her father.

She dreamed of a road trip with him. They'd spent so little time together since they moved to Grimm Falls and Cyn kept trying to be okay with it. Everyone grieved in their own way and avoidance was her father's way. But she wanted to remember her mother. She wanted to hear stories about her, and she thought her dad could jog her memory about her mother's laugh.

A couple months after Cyn's sixteenth birthday, Samantha went to New York to see to the construction of a new shop. Drew was busy with the police academy, and all the pieces fell into place. Cyn didn't want to make the trip alone, so she told her father a little lie.

She said it was a college scouting trip, and she kept up the ruse until they were halfway to Lisbon.

"What college is all the way out here?" her father asked with a curious chuckle. "Are you considering agricultural programs?"

"Actually," Cyn said, her heart climbing into her throat, "we're not going on a college tour. I want to visit mom's grave."

She saw the bulge of her father's eyes – sheer terror at the prospect – and she knew right then that she had made a mistake. She overestimated his ability to deal with this, and underestimated his dedication to avoiding the topic.

Cyn hurried to add, "I've been doing some reading about the stages of mourning and I think we both skipped some steps when we came to Grimm Falls. I thought it would be good for us to visit her."

"I can't," her father said. He looked like he might tear open the car door while the Beetle was hurtling down the highway at sixty miles an hour, so when he told her to pull over, she did. Then she watched him pace up and down on the side of the road in front of a soybean field for the next fifteen minutes.

She'd never seen her father have a panic attack before, and he hadn't had one since then.

"I just wanted to remember her," she said. "I thought we could share some memories while we drove. It's only thirty more minutes to the cemetery."

"No," her father said. "No, it's not a good idea. We need to go home."

"Daddy," Cyn said quietly, "I'm not going home until I do what I came for."

"I'm sorry, honey," he said, then he took out his phone and dialed the operator. "If you won't turn around, then I'm getting a cab back to Grimm Falls."

Cyn watched her father get into a yellow cab fifteen minutes later, then she continued to the cemetery alone. It was just as she remembered it – she might forget her mother's laugh, or the exact recipe for her sloppy joes, but the day of the funeral would be forever seared into Cyn's memory.

She stayed at her mother's grave for a long time. She'd picked up flowers from a gas station that she passed on her way through the quaint town of Lisbon, and lay them carefully at the base of the grave marker. Then she ran her fingers over the etched words carved into the gray stone.

Isabelle Robinson. Loving mother and wife. 1974 – 2007.

"Hi, Mama," Cyn said, tears threatening to choke her as she sat down cross-legged in front of the marker. She kept her hand on the stone. It was warm and Cyn knew it was just because it had been baking in the sun, but it helped her feel closer to her mother. Her words came out watery and unsteady. "I miss you so much. You told me to be good and I'm trying, but it's so hard. Samantha and Drew don't want me and I wish you were here."

Cyn stayed until dark, telling her mother everything that she couldn't bear to tell anyone else – how desperately she wanted to win her stepmother's approval and how disappointed she was in herself every time she failed to live up to Samantha's expectations of her. How she wished her father could be the smiling, spirited man that he was in her childhood. How the only person who she'd ever felt able to relate to, Marigold Grimm, had frozen her out after just a few weeks of friendship.

How, the older she got, the more Cyn wondered if Grimm Falls itself was rejecting her.

She put her hand on the marker again and asked, "Should I even go back? Or should I just keep driving until I find a new life somewhere else?"

She didn't expect an answer. She was talking to a stone, after all. But no sooner had the question left her mouth, a bird swooped down from a nearby hazel tree. Cyn ducked, shielding her face in alarm, and when she looked up again, the bird was sitting on her mother's grave marker.

Looking at her.

Its feathers were a beautiful, pure white and it cooed softly as it sat no more than two feet away from her. Cyn looked around the cemetery, but there was no one else there to witness it. Then she turned back to the bird and asked, "Mama?"

In a flutter of wings, it took flight again, disappearing back into the trees and leaving Cyn to feel rather foolish. *Thank god there was no one here to see that. They'd think I lost my marbles.* She gathered her wits about her and drove back to Grimm Falls, where Samantha was waiting to take away the pink Beetle. Cyn never saw it again.

❆

CYN DIDN'T HAVE much to say during dinner. Samantha's mention of the cemetery incident, as it had come to be known in their family, had put her in a brooding mood so she picked at her meal and watched Drew repeatedly run his index finger over the newly smooth patch on his bare chin.

At least he wasn't completely ignoring her warning.

"By the way, Cyn," Samantha announced as the waiter carried away their empty plates at the end of the meal, "I decided it would be wise to make a last-minute run to the New York boutique to make sure everything's in tip-top order the weekend before my Nylon photoshoot. As much as I'd love to meet your firefighter buddies, I won't be able to attend the service awards. Your father has agreed to take my place."

"Oh," Cyn said. "Okay."

Samantha loved to drop bombs like this on her at the last minute, and Cyn wondered why she couldn't have mentioned it privately. She looked at her father, wondering if he felt slighted because she hadn't asked him in the first place. She'd wanted to, but this event meant more to Samantha than it did to him.

"I'll be happy to go with you, pumpkin," Cyn's father said, and Samantha simply looked annoyed. She never liked it when Cyn and her father spent time together, ever since the cemetery incident, but in this case, her hands were tied – unless she wanted to force Drew to attend the event, and in that case, Cyn really would put her foot down.

Not on my watch.

When the meal was over, Cyn chased Drew into the parking lot. "Hey, wait a minute. Can we talk?"

Drew glared at her. "I thought we already did that."

"I was thinking about what you said at your apartment," Cyn said. "About how I stole your life. I understand how you could feel like that. I lost my father when he married your mother, and I know you feel the same way."

Drew scoffed at her. "Was that an apology? Because if so, it was the worst one I've ever heard."

Cyn's fists clenched involuntarily, then she worked at

uncurling them. Ten years was a long time to tiptoe around her stepbrother and she was so tired of it. She was ready to do whatever it took to smooth things over once and for all – and get him to stop being a menace to Grimm Falls and to Marigold. But it would be a cold day in hell before she apologized for doing her best to survive in a terrible set of circumstances.

She wanted to make all of it go away, once and for all, but she couldn't do that if she let Drew get under her skin.

"It's an acknowledgment," she said, hoping it would be enough. "I had an idea - a way to make things right between us."

"I'm listening," Drew said, crossing his arms over his chest.

"I know it was really hard on you when you couldn't finish the police academy," she said. *When you got kicked out of the academy because you've never taken anything seriously in your life,* was what she wanted to say, but that wouldn't serve her goal of building bridges, so she bit back the truth in favor of a softened version. "What if I could get you a job in the police department, as a dispatcher or something like that? I've got friends there and I bet I could pull a few strings to get you an interview."

"Why would you do that?" Drew asked.

"Because whether you like it or not, you're my brother," Cyn said. Then she took a deep breath and said what she really chased after him for. "And because if I do this for you, you have to promise there won't be any more fires. You're going to get caught sooner or later anyway, so just quit while you're ahead and I'll do what I can to help you with your career, okay?"

Drew narrowed his eyes at her and for a second, she thought she'd made a mistake. He was going to throw the offer back in her face and stubbornly insist on making his own way. But then he surprised her and said, "Fine."

"Good," Cyn answered. "I'll make the call tonight."

❉

SHE WENT STRAIGHT HOME and called Gus. Her palms were slick and she wondered if she was making the wrong decision, but this seemed like the best way for everyone to get what they wanted. Drew could live out his dream of being a police officer, at least to the extent that was possible without having graduated from the academy. Cyn would know that Grimm Falls was safe, and she could face Marigold again knowing that there was no further risk that Drew would take out his impotent rage on her poor garden again.

Gus, on the other hand, had been skeptical.

They talked for more than twenty minutes while he tried to figure out why Cyn was suddenly advocating for a step sibling that had never been anything but a terror to her.

"You remember the barn incident in your freshman year, right?" he asked. "He humiliated you, and that was far from the only time."

"I know," Cyn said. "He may not be blood, but he's family, and family always deserves another chance."

"No, they don't," Gus insisted. "You've done enough for them – more than enough."

Cyn pinched the bridge of her nose between her fingertips, staving off a headache. This conversation would be so much easier if she could explain the whole thing to Gus, but if he found out what she'd done, he wouldn't hesitate to bring Drew's name to Detective Holt. The investigation would turn on him and everything Cyn was trying to do to preserve the peace would be for nothing.

"Look, all I'm asking for is an interview," Cyn said. "If Drew blows it, then that's on him. Do you think you could talk to the police chief about it in the morning?"

"Fine, but I don't understand you," Gus said.

When Cyn hung up, she found a text message from Marigold that brought a smile to her lips.

The bluebells are thriving in their new plot. Can I take you out to dinner tomorrow night to thank you for them?

With that, the tone of the whole evening turned around. Cyn couldn't wipe the smile off her lips if she tried, and she sent back three words that made her stomach tingle with excitement and desire.

It's a date.

Then she stripped off her clothes and crawled naked between the sheets of her bed. It had been one of the longest and most taxing weeks of her life, and between the firehouse and her desire to fill up every spare moment that she could with Marigold, Cyn had hardly slept since the first fire at the museum.

She was asleep the moment her head hit the pillow, and in her dream, it was the night of the service awards. The Grimm House ballroom was decorated to the nines and the room was filled with row upon row of chairs. Every one of them was filled with important people from the city administration, and at the front of the room stood lovely Marigold in a shimmering silver evening gown.

She held a stack of envelopes in her hands – the names of all the award winners that would be announced that night – but when she looked out at the audience, her eyes rested solely on Cyn. When she leaned forward, her plump lips forming the name of the Firefighter of the Year, it was Cyn's name that she called.

The room erupted in polite applause and Cyn stood, floating more than walking as she made her way to the front of the room.

When she turned around to accept her award, she saw that she'd been wrong. The room was not quite full. There was a sea of faces she didn't recognize looking back at her, and at the very front of the crowd, there was a row of empty chairs with a banner draped across them – *reserved for the family of Cyn Robinson*.

When she turned again, Marigold was gone.

TWENTY-TWO
MARIGOLD

Mari picked Cyn up for their date in her emerald green BMW. They met at the firehouse at the end of Cyn's shift and when Cyn hopped in, she leaned across the gearshift to kiss Marigold. Then she asked, "So, where are we going?"

"I actually had an unconventional idea," Marigold said. "Do you know the teen center downtown?"

"The one that works with underprivileged youth?" Cyn asked. "Yeah, my crew got called out there about six months ago when they were doing a cooking class for the kids and they took a little detour into the art of flambé."

Mari laughed, then said, "I've been volunteering there over the last couple of summers to teach the kids about container gardening. I'm due to drop by again and I thought if you liked the idea, we could go together and harvest some veggies."

"Sounds good," Cyn said, "although I'm sure you'll

be teaching me just as much as the kids. I'm not sure I've got a green thumb."

"You will if you keep seeing me," Marigold said. "I'll get you up to speed."

"Let's do it, then," Cyn said. She slipped her hand into Mari's as she drove down the road. When Marigold pulled into the small parking lot behind the teen center – an unassuming cinderblock building – Cyn asked, "Can I tell you something honestly?"

"Anything," Marigold said.

Cyn looked serious, taking her hand back. For an instant, Mari felt nervous. Then Cyn said, "I was a little worried about going on a date with you. You're Grimm Falls royalty and I was picturing a fancy restaurant with a thousand forks to choose from. This is much more my speed."

"Well, I was planning to take you to the fancy restaurant after we finished up here," Mari said, "but if you'd prefer, we can just go get a pizza instead."

"I'd like that," Cyn said.

They went inside, where Marigold introduced Cyn to the center director, Garrett, and his second in command, a raven-haired woman named Kiera. Kiera led them through the building and out a side door, where there was a small patio with about a dozen twelve-inch pots brimming over with greenery.

"Wow, I'm impressed," Cyn said. "This looks like a whole salad worth of veggies."

There were ripe cherry tomatoes and bush beans, plus a large head of lettuce and some small red peppers, as well as a whole host of herbs. Kiera was beaming as she said, "The kids really get into this every year. They'll be excited that it's finally harvest time – they're just finishing up the after-school activity, so I'll go gather them up, okay?"

"Thanks," Mari said. As soon as Kiera was gone and they were alone on the patio, Cyn put her hands on Mari's waist and pulled her close.

"You're incredible," she said. "I didn't think it was possible to like you more than I already did, but then I find out stuff like this. How is that you're so amazing?"

"Just lucky, I guess," Marigold said with a small laugh.

They had a few minutes before the kids were ready to come outside to the garden, and Cyn had no problem finding something to fill the time. She pressed Marigold up against a small potting bench, her fingers caressing Marigold's curls as their hips sought each other. It felt so good – so right – to be with Cyn, but in the back of her mind, Mari couldn't stop thinking about her father's retirement.

Was all this a brief detour on her way to the conservatorship?

When she heard footsteps approaching inside the building, Marigold pushed Cyn away, and then the steel door opened and a dozen kids crowded onto the patio. Mari taught them how to harvest what was ripe and Cyn jumped in wherever she could help. They divided it all up to take home, and the whole time, Marigold kept stealing glances at Cyn. She got lost in the work easily despite her protestations that she was inexperienced in the garden, and Mari was just as intrigued by her as she'd been when they first met as kids.

Was there a way she could have it all?

❄

THE FOLLOWING AFTERNOON, Marigold sat across from her father at their usual table in the outdoor area of the Red Hen restaurant. Her father was never one for outdoor dining, preferring the modern luxury of temperature control and an absence of insects, but he also wasn't a man who was in the habit of saying no to his only daughter's wishes. At least, not very often.

Marigold enjoyed the patio of the Red Hen because of the beautiful display of lush ferns circling the dining area. Today, she wasn't paying much attention to the greenery.

This was Mari's first one-on-one meeting with her father since the retirement party, and it was all she could do not to demand answers the moment she sat down. She had to keep reminding herself that he'd never promised her anything, and that it was possible her expectations had ballooned beyond what they should have been in her frenzy to make the event perfect.

Her father didn't make her wait too long. The waiter came by to drop off their drinks – the peach Bellinis that they'd become accustomed to in the summertime and which were now starting to wear on Mari in her impatience. Then her father said, "The retirement party was wonderful. You did a fantastic job, even with the extenuating circumstances."

"Thank you," Marigold said. Then with a hopeful smile, she asked, "Does that mean you'll stop trying to force Ryan on me as a partner?"

She hoped the smile would lighten the tone of her question, but her father wasn't amused. He frowned and said, "I'm not trying to force anything on you, princess. I just keep hoping you'll see my point about accepting help so that you're not tethered to the house all the time. Ryan could be a real asset to you if you allowed him to be."

Marigold rolled her eyes. "I know you like him, and he's good at his job. But I really think I can handle the estate on my own."

"It's not a question of your abilities," her father said, setting down his Bellini flute. "Princess, I hope you don't take this as too harsh a criticism, but you can be so bullheaded sometimes. I know you *can* run the estate yourself, but I don't think it's wise. What about Cynthia Robinson?"

Marigold was taken aback. She expected to hear pushback from her father today, but she never expected to hear that name on his lips. "What about her?"

He gave Mari a knowing look, then said, "I saw you sneaking off with her at the party."

"I was just showing her the library," Marigold said. It was true, if only a half-truth.

"Emily tells me you two are dating," her father said, and Mari flushed with a wave of embarrassment. She'd never had this type of conversation with her father before and it was just as mortifying as the teenaged Marigold had imagined. "Don't blame Emily. She's just looking out for your best interest, the same as I am. Do you care about this girl, Cynthia?"

"She goes by Cyn," Mari corrected. Then she smiled involuntarily as she answered, "Yes, I do. It's only been a week but I've never felt this way about anyone before."

"All the more reason to take a partner who can share the responsibility of running the estate," her father said. "Princess, I did it alone for twenty-five years, but that's because the house kept me busy. It kept me from missing your mother too much, but when I look back on my career, I think it would have been nice if I'd had more time to spend with you. Don't follow in my footsteps just because you think it's a badge of honor to carry all that weight yourself. If you care about Cyn, give the relationship an opportunity to grow. Don't miss the forest for the trees."

"I just don't think Ryan is the right person to share that responsibility," Marigold hedged. Her father was making a lot of sense, and she had found herself increasingly distracted over the past week thanks to Cyn's new presence in her life. But all she'd wanted since she was young was to run Grimm House, and to honor her family history. "He's so stuck on the financial side of things. Did you know last week he told me the foyer would look more modern if we painted the original wood trim a lighter color?"

Her father laughed at the horrified look on her face, then said, "I never said it had to be Ryan. Hold job interviews. Find a partner who's right for you. Emily has more practical experience than business sense, but she might be a good fit for you."

Mari sat back in her chair and sipped her Bellini. That was an idea.

The waiter came back and took their orders – Marigold liked to order off the seasonal menu and she picked a squash ravioli while her father ordered the same fresh vegetable omelet that he always had. Then while they were waiting for their meals, Marigold pulled a copy of the police sketch she'd made from her purse.

Cyn had told her the face didn't ring a bell with her or any of the other firefighters, and no one on the Grimm House staff recognized the man, either. Marigold's father was her last hope.

She unfolded the page and handed it to him, asking, "Does this man look familiar to you?"

"Let's see," her father said, pulling a pair of reading glasses out of the inside pocket of his suit jacket. He studied the paper carefully, then after a minute, he handed it back to her with a frown and said, "No, princess, I'm afraid he doesn't. Is he supposed to?"

"Not necessarily," Marigold said. "That's the man I saw in the garden on the morning of the fire. The sketch artist told me I should show it to everyone, but so far no one knows who it is. I thought it could be someone you've met through Grimm House, a business contact."

"I don't recognize him," her father said. "Although, what's that on his chin? A mole, maybe?"

"I'm not sure," Mari said. "It was so dark, I didn't get

a good look at him. That's the only distinguishing characteristic I could remember, and I don't remember it well."

"Whatever it is, I bet it won't be hard to spot," her father said.

Marigold folded the sketch and put it back in her purse, and the waiter came by again not long after with their meals. While they ate, her father kept smiling at Marigold until she began to suspect that the Bellini had gone to his head. "What?"

"Tell me about your girlfriend," he said. "I'm so happy you've found someone."

"It's really new, and I wouldn't say she's my girlfriend yet," Marigold hedged. It seemed almost superstitious to say she was, especially when their fate was still up in the air. And yet, she liked the sound of it. What would her life look like if Cyn Robinson really was her girlfriend? Finally, Marigold allowed herself to just be happy and not question it as she said, "She's really great. I like her a lot."

TWENTY-THREE
CYN

For their next date, Marigold invited Cyn over to Grimm House a few days after their visit to the teen center. The estate was bustling with activity when she arrived, as Marigold's staff prepared the amphitheater for a late-summer concert.

Cyn had felt conflicted about seeing Mari ever since she discovered the identity of the arsonist who torched her beloved garden. She knew she should tell Marigold the truth, but she also knew there was a good chance it would ruin the incredible thing that was growing between them. She'd waited ten years to feel this way, so she did her best to suppress her concerns every time Marigold wanted to see her.

When she met Mari in the foyer, Marigold looked anxious and a momentary panic rippled through Cyn. *Does she know?*

"What's wrong?" she asked.

"Nothing," Mari said. "It's just that I'm usually the

one who's in charge of making sure the summer concerts are set up and ready to go."

"You want to be out there, double-checking everything and making sure it's all coming together, don't you?" Cyn asked.

"My assistant, Emily, has everything under control," Mari said, not sounding quite as confident as her words intended. "I'm treating this as a trial run to find out if I can handle stepping back a little, and to find out if Emily likes the increased responsibility. She's handled plenty of other concerts and she'll find me if there's trouble, but tonight is about us. I thought we could make a picnic and take it down to the garden – we'll be able to hear the concert from there, but it'll also give us a little privacy from the crowd."

"I like that," Cyn said, sliding her arm around Marigold and giving her a kiss. *Just relax and enjoy the time you have together,* she told herself, then she asked, "Who's playing?"

"It's an all-female Grateful Dead tribute band," Mari said, and Cyn's eyes lit up before she even finished talking.

"The Scarlet Begonias," Cyn said. "They play the bar circuit downtown. I love them."

"Well then, it's a date," Marigold said. She kissed Cyn back, then led her to the staircase. "Come on, we'll go up to my quarters and make a picnic basket."

Mari brought Cyn up to the third floor, where her quarters comprised one wing of the estate and the rest of the staff quarters took up the rest of the floor. She gave

Cyn a short tour, looking self-conscious as Cyn took in the enormous space.

The ceilings were twelve feet high, with intricate crown molding all around. There was a formal sitting room with a large stone fireplace as well as a cozier, but still quite large, living room. Heavy velvet drapes hung from all the windows and every inch of Marigold's living quarters was elaborately decorated and meticulously clean.

"I didn't design it," she explained as they walked past a large bedroom. "My father hired a decorator when I was a kid and when he moved out, it just wasn't very high on my priority list to make the space my own."

"You live here alone?" Cyn asked as she paused in the doorway to the bedroom. Marigold's bed was a four-poster that stood importantly in the center of the room, and there were dark wood dressers and armoires against the walls. The very sight of the bed made Cyn's heart beat a little faster as she wondered where this date might end.

"I do," Mari confirmed. "But I'm hardly ever here – I mostly just come up here to shower and sleep."

"I can think of at least one more thing we could do," Cyn said. She caught Marigold around the waist and ran her fingers through her wavy locks as she kissed her. The Scarlet Begonias' first warm-up notes floated in through an open window and Cyn asked, "Should we get that picnic packed?"

"If you insist," Mari said, grinning.

She brought Cyn to the kitchen, which had marble

countertops and custom cabinetry, as well as top of the line appliances and the biggest refrigerator Cyn had ever seen outside of a professional kitchen. *If this is the lifestyle Mari's used to, I don't ever want her to see my place,* she thought as Mari went over to the fridge and pulled out a couple blocks of cheese.

"Smoked gouda or aged cheddar?" Mari asked.

"Both," Cyn said. Mari pointed her to a wicker basket on the end of the counter and Cyn took over packing everything as Mari gathered it from the fridge and cupboards. There were the cheeses, plus a hard salami, a pack of rosemary crackers, and a bottle of red wine. When Cyn explained that she didn't drink, Mari swapped it out for a couple bottles of sparkling water, then she set a couple of plates and a pair of cloth napkins on the counter. Cyn carefully packed it all, then picked up the basket and offered Marigold her elbow. "Shall we?"

"Yes," Marigold said, pressing her body against Cyn's so that her hips hit the counter as they shared another long kiss. How could she tell Mari her secret when she stood to lose so much?

Marigold grabbed a blanket from a large closet in her bedroom, then Cyn followed her down to the garden. They ducked under the caution tape and went past the burned-up section at the entrance, then Marigold brought her to a lush green space that Cyn hadn't been to before. It was lit up with string lights and in the distance, the Scarlet Begonias were just ramping up with a soulful rendition of Box of Rain.

It was a perfect night – one that Cyn had dreamed of for a long time – and she wasn't enjoying it as much as she wanted to. Not with her information about Drew weighing on her chest.

She'd hoped that getting Drew a better job and securing his promise to stop setting fires would be enough. If she could protect Grimm Falls – and Marigold – from her stepbrother, she could keep his secret.

But she hadn't been able to shake the fear that he was lying to her, or that he'd mess up his interview, or even worse – that her relationship with Marigold would continue beyond her wildest dreams, she'd bring her home to meet her family someday, and the moment Mari met Drew, she'd know him from the police sketch she'd made. Even without the soul patch, the resemblance was clear.

How hurt would she feel if Cyn had known all along and never said anything?

Marigold lay out a blanket on a flat patch of grass in a small clearing of the garden, with tall wildflowers rising on three sides of them. It was a thick flannel one that she'd pulled out of her closet and it was soft as they sat down. Cyn set the picnic basket on the edge of the blanket and as they sat back to listen to the music, Mari sat with her hips touching Cyn's, her body nestled into the crook of Cyn's arm.

She had to tell Marigold what she knew before she fell any deeper in love with her.

It's all a dream we dreamed one afternoon long ago. Cyn picked up the words to the song, the vocals carrying crystal clear across the grounds. When Marigold noticed the direction of her attention, she said, "It's nice, isn't it? Sometimes when I'm working late, I like to open the window in my office and listen to the concerts from there."

"It's beautiful," Cyn said, then let out a sigh. She didn't want to ruin the moment before they'd even had a chance to eat, but would the news go over any better on a full stomach? Better to get it over with. "I have to tell you something. It's about your garden."

"Did the fire inspector find a lead?" Mari asked, hopeful.

"No," Cyn said. "In fact, he doesn't know this information."

She felt sick. Why couldn't she just keep bottling this up and enjoy a night with the beautiful Marigold Grimm? It was a fantasy come true and she was about to ruin the whole thing.

"I'm sorry," she said. "I've been twisting myself in knots for days over whether I should tell you. I think I have to, but I'm afraid."

"Afraid of what?" Marigold asked. It was just light enough thanks to the string lights for Cyn to see the confused expression on Mari's face. The way she knit her brows together when she was anxious was endearing – everything about her was.

"Afraid you'll be upset and I will have ruined what's been building between us, which I've really enjoyed," Cyn said. "And I'm also afraid that you'll take the information and give it to Detective Holt."

Marigold narrowed her eyes. "Are you trying to protect someone? Please don't tell me *you* set my garden on fire."

"No," Cyn hurried to say. "God, no... but I'm pretty certain my stepbrother did."

She looked into the tightly growing wildflowers while Friend of the Devil played through the air. *I set out running but I'll take my time. A friend of the devil is a friend of mine.* Then Marigold asked, "How do you know?"

"That police sketch," Cyn said. "I'm so sorry I lied to you, but as soon as I looked at it, I saw Drew. Then I went to his apartment and he had a pack of cigarettes that matched the brand of the one we found in your garden. I confronted him about it and he didn't confess, but he may as well have."

"Why didn't you go to the police?" Marigold asked. "Or tell me when you figured it out?"

"He's family," Cyn said.

"He's a criminal," Marigold shot back. "And you told me yourself, he treats you like shit."

"I know," Cyn said, hanging her head. She felt like her heart was being physically pulled in two different directions, and even as she confessed all of this to Marigold, she didn't know which side to choose. A family that didn't respect her, but had always been there for her, or a new relationship that might blossom into something beautiful, or might not?

"You have to go to the fire inspector," Marigold urged

her. "What if he sets another fire? He could hurt someone."

"I made him promise me that the fires would end," Cyn said. "That's why I got him the job interview. It'll make us even, at least in his eyes - no more competition."

Mari gave her a cynical look. Cyn held her breath, and then Marigold said, "Come on, Cyn. You know that's not going to work, right?"

"It's a long shot," she said. "I know that. But my stepmother dislikes me enough as it is. If I'm the reason her son gets arrested, she'll never speak to me again – probably won't let me near my dad, either."

"You wouldn't be the reason," Marigold said. "Drew set those fires, and family or not, it isn't your responsibility to cover for him."

"I know you're right," Cyn said. She tried to imagine herself walking into the police station and turning her stepbrother in, but she couldn't see it. "I've been covering for Drew for years. He does something awful, usually to me, and I can't tell anyone because I know it'll make the whole situation ten times worse."

"You told me," Marigold said softly. "That's a step in the right direction."

"Maybe," Cyn said. "You're sure you're not mad?"

"Not at you," Mari said. She tucked a wild strand of Cyn's hair behind her ear, then said, "Should we eat this picnic before the cheese gets soft?"

"Sure," Cyn said. She felt a wave of relieve, almost literally washing over her. She'd told Marigold the worst secret she had and Mari was still sitting next to her on the picnic blanket, looking at her with the same seductive blue eyes as she had before she knew. They were going to get past this after all. As Cyn pulled out the two bottles of sparkling water, she asked, "Can I tell you the story of why I don't drink?"

She wasn't sure what made her bring it up. It wasn't a story she'd ever told before – not even to Gus. But now that she'd begun unburdening her soul to Marigold, she wanted to keep going.

"Please," Mari said.

"I was a sophomore in high school," Cyn said while Marigold unpacked the basket. "Although I never really got the hang of making friends here, other than my best buddy, Gus. Drew had a few good friends and I was still very committed to making at least one member of my new family like me. It was spring and Samantha had just taken my car away a few months before – that's a whole other story that I'll tell you another time, but suffice it to say we weren't talking at the time. Drew decided to skip his senior prom and hang out with his friends instead, and I was the only one he confided in about that plan. When he invited me to come along, I was over the moon. I thought it meant he was finally going to give the whole sibling thing a try. Well, I guess he did, if you consider hazing to be a typical sibling activity."

"Oh no," Marigold said. "What happened?"

"You know that barn that burned down last week? It was in the newspapers."

"Yeah," Marigold said. "The one on County Route 10."

"That's the one," Cyn answered. She rolled her eyes and said, "I should have known Drew was the arsonist as soon as I responded to that fire. It was a popular place with the cool, edgy kids when we were in school, and I imagine it still was up until it got turned into a pile of ash. Anyway, Drew always wanted to go and he never got invited – he didn't hang out in the right crowds. So when everyone else was at prom, he decided that was going to be his time to make some memories at the barn. He took me, a couple of guys from his class – you might have known them but I don't remember their names – and a bottle of Jack Daniels. I didn't know he had the alcohol until we got there and he pulled it out of the trunk of his car. I think he swiped it from my father's wet bar. I had never drank alcohol before that night, and I haven't touched a drop of the stuff since. Just thinking about it makes me want to gag a little bit."

"You got pretty drunk, huh?" Marigold asked as she set the cheese and salami out on a plate, then opened the box of crackers.

"That's putting it mildly," Cyn said. "Drew started right in with a round of shots. I drank mine and it felt like fire going all the way down my esophagus and landing like a bomb in my stomach. I managed to keep it down – I still think that was a miracle – and then he gave me another. I tried to refuse it but he said I could either drink the whiskey or I could walk home. I drank it and then sat there trying not to vomit for the next ten minutes while Drew and his friends explored the barn. When they came back, Drew gave me another shot and I took it because it was at least five miles back into town and I didn't even have a cell phone at the time so I could call a cab. I stood up and decided to walk around a bit, try and walk off the nausea, and that's when the alcohol hit me. When people say it goes to your head, I don't think they have anything as severe in mind as what I experienced. The whole world tipped sideways – I could feel the ground moving under my feet – and then it all went black. When I woke up, I had no idea how much time passed or what else had happened. Drew and his friends were gone and there was vomit in my hair – Samantha used to make me wear it long back then. I cut it all off myself the very next day."

"So he left you there?"

"Yeah," Cyn said. "It took me three hours to walk home because I was still drunk and the world was spinning around me for the first hour. I'm lucky I didn't get hit by a car or something. When I finally did get home, it was close to dawn and I found a note from Drew on my pillow. *You were home all night. I went to a concert in Granville with some friends.* When I dragged myself to breakfast a few hours later, he was telling Samantha a story about hitting a deer on his way home from seeing the Black Keys. I never did find out what he really hit, but I lied for him and corroborated his story because there was no point in Samantha hating both of us."

Marigold set down the knife she was using to cut the wax off the gouda. She turned her full attention to Cyn and said, "Drew is an asshole who only cares about himself. You have to turn him in. Promise me."

"Are you going to tell the police what I said?" Cyn asked. She was feeling anxious again – it had felt so good to stop holding those secrets, but had it been a mistake to trust Marigold after all?

"I won't tell them," she said, "*if* you promise to do it yourself. A secret like that's not worth keeping. He could set another fire and really hurt someone."

Cyn let out a deep sigh. Once again, she knew that Marigold was right, but ten years of trying desperately to keep the peace in her unstable family wasn't easily undone by the simple urge to do what was right.

"Okay," she said. "I'll go in the morning and talk to Detective Holt."

"Good," Mari said. She pulled Cyn into a long hug, stroking her hair and making her feel safe while the Scarlet Begonias played their namesake song in the distance. *Once in a while you get shown the light in the strangest of places if you look at it right.*

"Come on," Marigold said after the song ended. "Let's eat."

❄

THEY LAY down on the picnic blanket after they were finished with the cheese and crackers. Mari put her head in the crook of Cyn's arm and they stared up at the stars above them while the Scarlet Begonias continued their set, and after a while, Cyn's eyelids began to grow heavy.

She must have drifted into sleep because she found herself in the grand ballroom after a while, and the room looked drastically different from the last time she was there. There were many chairs set up in rows and the podium was standing at the front of the room – she was at the service awards again.

People began to appear in the seats while Cyn stood in the aisle, and Marigold went to the podium. She called Cyn's name and Cyn looked anxiously for her family in the crowd. They were there – no embarrassingly empty seats this time – but when she got to the podium, Mari ripped the award out of her hands and the whole room erupted in an angry round of booing.

Cyn twitched awake just as the audience was standing up, beginning to close in on her at the podium, and Marigold asked, "Did you have a bad dream?"

"No," she lied, and Mari saw right through it.

She bent over and kissed Cyn's temple, then took her hand and helped her to her feet. "Come on, the concert's over. Let's go to bed."

TWENTY-FOUR
MARIGOLD

Marigold brought Cyn back upstairs and led her by the hand into her bedroom. They crawled into the four-poster bed together and made love slowly, invigorated by the short nap they'd taken in the garden. Then when they were finally spent, they settled into each other's arms and Cyn was asleep again immediately.

Mari had a harder time falling asleep. This was a kind of intimacy that she'd never experienced before and she wanted to enjoy every minute of it. She loved the rise and fall of Cyn's chest and the sound of her heart beating in Marigold's ear. She loved the way their bodies were cradled together, their curves fitting perfectly against each other.

And against all her protestations about being sole conservator of Grimm House, she loved the feeling of having nowhere else to be and nothing she'd rather be doing.

She'd approached Emily about the possibility of

becoming co-conservator after her lunch meeting with her father. Emily was just an assistant, but she'd been at Marigold's side ever since she started working full-time after college and she knew the estate's affairs inside and out. She might not understand the history of Grimm House the way that Marigold and her father did, but she respected it and she worked hard.

"It would be a lot more work," Marigold had told her, "but it would come with a very nice salary increase."

"You're thinking about relinquishing control?" Emily had asked, incredulous. "Marigold Grimm is considering the idea of having a partner?"

In more ways than one, Mari had thought.

"Not relinquishing," she said. That word sounded too severe – too hands-off. "I trust you and I know you take pride in your work, but it's a big job and I want you to be sure it's something that you want."

She'd suggested the Scarlet Begonias concert as a trial run, much like the retirement party had been a trial run for Marigold. She would need to sit down with Emily in the morning and ask her how it had gone, but from her vantage point in the garden, it all seemed to go off without a hitch.

She snuggled against Cyn and closed her eyes at last. She was on the verge of having it all.

❄

THE NEXT MORNING, Marigold woke up a few minutes before Cyn. She lay still so as not to disturb her, and when Cyn stirred, Mari sat up and watched Cyn stretch and wipe the sleep from her eyes. Even that was the most charming thing Marigold had ever seen. She leaned forward and kissed Cyn's forehead, then asked, "Did you sleep well?"

"Surprisingly, yes," Cyn said. "I thought I wouldn't be able to sleep knowing what's on the agenda for today, but you make me feel at home."

She wrapped her arms around Marigold's waist and squeezed her tight, then nuzzled her face into the side of Mari's neck. Her breath was hot against Marigold's skin and it stirred desire in her, followed by a rush of adrenaline.

"Cyn?"

"Hmm?"

"Never mind," she said, pushing Cyn's head back down til her lips met her collarbone. She'd been thinking about the conversation she'd had with her father the other day, when he called Cyn her girlfriend. She was about to ask, but it was too soon – that would be crazy.

"I'm afraid I can't do that," Cyn said, raising her head and grinning at Mari. "Now you've got me curious."

With trepidation, Marigold asked, "Do you believe in love at first sight?"

She could hardly believe her own ears. After a lifetime of choosing work over relationships, it seemed like the most ridiculous question she could ask, but as she lay in Cyn's arms, waiting for her to wake up, Marigold couldn't think of a better place to call heaven.

She waited for Cyn to laugh at her, like Marigold

probably would have if the question had been reversed. But Cyn surprised her, like she often did. "Absolutely."

"Really?"

"Yeah," Cyn said. "My parents are a perfect example."

"Your father and stepmother?" Mari asked.

"Lord, no," Cyn said with a snort. "I'm talking about my dad and my real mother. They met in college – she was a poet and he was getting his MBA, and they ran into each other in the student union. She asked him to a poetry reading and he went even though he'd never voluntarily heard a poem in his life, and they fell in love that very night. They were married by the end of the school year and everyone in their lives thought they were nuts, but the just *knew*." She cracked a smile and kissed Marigold, then added, "And I knew from the moment I saw you in that ice cream parlor ten years ago."

"You did?" Mari asked.

She felt even more adrenaline coursing through her veins now than when she'd been waiting for her father to make his announcement at the retirement party. Blood was rushing to her head and she thought she might either burst into happy tears or pass out from the overwhelming emotion.

"Does that scare you?" Cyn asked.

"A little," Marigold admitted. "I don't know how I could possibly live up to expectations that you've been holding on to for that long."

"Love doesn't come with expectations," Cyn said. "And if it did, you would have surpassed them all."

Marigold's heart was pounding nearly visibly in her chest and she asked, "Will you be my girlfriend?"

"I thought you'd never ask," Cyn said.

Then she pulled Marigold down to the mattress with a delighted yelp and pushed her nightgown up her thighs. Marigold closed her eyes as Cyn inched her legs apart and slid her hand into the wetness waiting for her. As the first shiver of pleasure ran through her, she thought, *So this is love.*

❆

THEY MADE love once in the bed, then again while they made a very cursory attempt to take a shower together and instead succumbed to their desires. Then Marigold brought Cyn downstairs and asked Federico to make them a breakfast omelet to share. They ate on the terrace, and when their plates were clean, Cyn set down her fork and said, "Well, I think I've put off this morning's task as long as I can. I better go into town and talk to Detective Holt."

"Do you want me to go with you?" Marigold asked. "I can provide moral support."

"No," Cyn said. "Thank you, but I think I need to do this alone."

"Okay," Mari said. "Call me when you're finished and I'll find a way to make you feel better."

She gave Cyn a flirtatious look – she was really enjoying her newfound confidence, even more now that she could call Cyn her girlfriend. Cyn kissed her, then headed to her truck parked in the gravel drive. There weren't many other cars in the lot – it was a slow day for Grimm House and Marigold had plenty of work to catch up on after all the time she'd taken off to be with Cyn.

First, she found Emily in the kitchen, finalizing the menu for a wedding they'd be hosting in a few weeks' time.

"Is that for the Thomas wedding?" she asked as she came over to the prep area where Emily and Federico were talking.

"Sure is," Emily said. "I wanted to talk to you about that - they were supposed to have their ceremony in the garden, but I'm not sure we'll be ready in time. Maybe we can move them to the terrace instead."

"No," Mari said. "They want to use the pergola as their altar."

"It's only three weeks from now," Emily pointed out. "And everything's still-"

"Don't say it," Mari interrupted her. She couldn't stand to hear those words again – *blackened, charred, burned, drowned.* Then she smiled and said, "I guess it's a good thing I already placed an order with Green Thumb to replace the stuff that was ruined. They're coming this afternoon to deliver the first batch of replacement plants. We'll be ready for the Thomases, I promise."

"Okay," Emily said, sounding unsure.

"Can I talk to you in the parlor when you're done with the menu?" Mari asked. Emily agreed and Marigold went into the parlor. When Em came into the room, she asked her about the concert. "How did it go? Did you like being in charge?"

"I did, actually," Emily said. "And everything went smoothly, although I have to confess I was dying to come up with a problem just so I could spy on your date. How are things going with Cyn?"

Marigold attempted to suppress her smile, but it only worked for a fraction of a second before she was filled to bursting and she said, "It's official – she's my girlfriend."

"Wow," Emily said, her eyes going wide. "That's fast!"

"It's crazy, I know," Mari started to say, thinking of what Cyn told her about her parents and all the people who thought they were moving too fast. But then Em threw her arms around her.

"Whatever – if you know, you know," she said. "I'm happy for you."

"Thank you," Marigold said, giving in to the hug. When she released her, she turned serious again and said, "This estate means a lot to me, but I really don't want to screw up what I've got with Cyn. If you want the job, I'd love for you to be my co-conservator. You don't have to make a decision right away-"

"What's there to think about?" Emily asked. "You know I love Grimm House. I'd be honored." They hugged again, then Emily laughed and added, "Now you just have to break the news to Ryan. He's going to be crushed."

"I know," Mari said. "I think I'm going to wait until

tomorrow. Today's been too nice to ruin it with that conversation."

※

WHEN MARIGOLD'S plants were delivered in the early afternoon, she changed into a pair of jeans and a T-shirt, then went downstairs. She had a plan, as always – she'd finish the job that the fire had started and tear out everything that was dead, then dig up the dirt that had been poisoned by the gasoline and replace it with fresh, nutrient-rich soil. She'd ordered hearty hostas and a large bag full of perennial bulbs, along with a load of fresh soil. All of that could go in the ground and safely take root before the first frost of autumn. Everything else would have to wait until spring.

Mari carried the hostas and bulbs to the greenhouse at the back of the estate for storage until she was ready for them. Then she retrieved a pair of gardening gloves, a shovel, and a wheelbarrow.

It hurt her soul to be carrying such blunt instruments into the garden – it was like she was preparing to dig a grave, not make something beautiful. But the damage had been done, and now it was necessary to dig out the poison so she could move on.

She spent the afternoon uprooting charred and withered plants, dumping them into the wheelbarrow and hauling them to a compost heap tucked discretely away in the back of the garden.

Mari kept her phone in her pocket with the ringer

turned up, waiting for Cyn's call and wondering how the conversation with Detective Holt was going. When she heard footsteps crunching on the gravel behind her, she wondered if Cyn decided to just come back without calling first and her heart skipped a beat at the prospect of seeing her again.

When she turned around, she saw her father instead.

He was grinning at her as he asked, "Are you aware that you're covered head to toe in dirt?"

Marigold looked down and saw that she was, in fact, filthy. Her white t-shirt was now anything but, and dirt stuck to the sweat on her forearms. She smiled back and said, "I guess I got a little lost in my work. To be fair, most of this is soot from the fire, not dirt."

"I haven't seen you get this dirty since you were a little girl," her father pointed out. It was true – normally, Marigold worked meticulously and even her gardening gloves remained clean. "What inspired this?"

"I just wanted to get all the burned-up plants out of the way as quickly as possible," Mari said. "I don't want to see the garden torn up like this any longer than I have to."

She took off her gloves and brushed the dirt from her arms and shirt as best she could, then she explained her plans for the garden and the impending wedding that she'd need to get it into shape for. "I'd like to watch someone get married here as soon as possible to lay down a happy memory on top of the bad one."

"That will be nice, princess," her father said. "Do you have a moment to talk? I came with some news."

"Of course," Marigold said. She set down her shovel and suggested that they go over to the meditation labyrinth.

As she guided her father through the garden, he looked around with wonder in his eyes and said, "I'm realizing now that I haven't spent any considerable time in the garden for some years. I remember when your mother started it, the garden was nothing more than a simple plot of vegetables about twelve feet square. You've done a lot to expand it."

"I try to add one new feature every year," Mari said as they came to the large, circular path of paving stones that she'd used to form her meditation labyrinth. "I built this with the help of the landscapers in my senior year of college. It's supposed to help you think."

"Does it work?" her father asked.

"I think so," Mari said.

They began to trace the path at a meandering pace and finally, her father came to the point. "I've set a date for my retirement."

Marigold's ears perked up, but she kept her eyes on the path in front of her. "Oh?"

"I'm ready now, and more importantly, I think you're ready now," he said. "I'm handing over the reins to you, effective at the beginning of the next financial quarter. The estate is yours, as are the staff. Choose a co-conservator or manage the place on your own – I'm sure you'll do great either way."

Marigold couldn't hide her feelings any longer. She jumped up and threw her arms around her father's neck like a teenage girl instead of the twenty-five-year-old, newly appointed estate conservator that she was. "Thank you. I won't disappoint you."

"I know you won't, princess," he said.

They kept walking, and then she said, "I've been thinking a lot about what you said regarding work-life balance, and I think you're right. I spoke to Emily this morning and asked her to work beside me. Ryan's a great marketing director and if he wants to stay on in that capacity, I'll be happy to work with him, but Emily will be a dedicated conservator and a good partner."

"I think that's a wonderful solution," her father said. He rested his hand approvingly on her shoulder, then directed his attention to the labyrinth path and asked, "So what's the point of this thing, anyway? To go in circles?"

"To find inner peace," Marigold said, laughing at his incredulous tone.

TWENTY-FIVE
CYN

Going to the police station to tell Detective Holt about Drew was one of the most terrifying and shameful moments of Cyn's life. She knew that everything Marigold told her the night before was true. None of this was her fault... so why did it feel like such an unforgivable betrayal of her family?

To go inside was to ruin Drew's life, but to turn around and run was to ruin any chance she might have of making a life with Marigold. She wanted to be someone Marigold deserved, not someone who protected a criminal family member who didn't care about her anyway.

Drew got himself into this, she reminded herself as she walked into the station. She was trying to turn it into a mantra that would get her through the meeting with Holt. *It's not my fault.*

Her stomach was tying itself in knots when she walked up to Marcy at the front desk and asked, "Is

Detective Holt here? I have some information about the arson case that he's working on."

"Yeah, he's in his office. You're from the fire department, right?" Marcy asked. Cyn nodded, so she told Cyn to go on back, then buzzed her through the secured door that led to the rest of the station.

She saw Gus sitting at his desk in the bullpen, along with a few other officers getting caught up on their paperwork. He had his head down and she walked briskly past him. She'd just got done begging him to pull strings and get her stepbrother an interview – if she had to dodge questions from him, she might not have the courage to keep going to the fire investigator's office.

Luckily, he was absorbed in his work and didn't notice her. She continued down the hall and with a heavy heart, she knocked on the door frame of Detective Holt's office.

He looked up from a mountain of paperwork and smiled. "Robinson. What can I do for you?"

"Sir, I have some information about the arson case," she said. "May I come in?"

"Sure, have a seat," Holt said. She took one more glance down the hall and her heart skipped a beat as she locked eyes with Gus. He'd heard her name and now he was giving her a goofball look – he had no idea why she was here.

Cyn stepped into the office and closed the door behind her.

As she sank into a chair across from Holt's desk, he reached for a thin folder and opened it on top of all the rest of his paperwork. He scanned through it – all the information they had so far about the three incidents – and said with a frown, "Looks like we don't have much. Braden Fox turned out to be a dead end, and nobody's recognized the man in our police sketch yet."

Cyn swallowed hard and said what she came for. "That's why I'm here - I recognize him."

Detective Holt gave her a surprised look. "Oh yeah?"

She wanted to fix her eyes on the corner of Holt's desk – anywhere other than his face. But she was here in a professional capacity as well as a family member of the perpetrator. She forced herself to look Detective Holt in the eyes as she said, "It's my stepbrother, Drew. Uh, that's Andrew Zeller."

Holt narrowed his eyes at her, leaning across the desk as he asked, "Why do you think that?"

Cyn sighed and pulled her phone out of her pocket, flipping through her photos until she found one of Drew – before he shaved the fuzz from his chin. She held it up for Detective Holt and he compared it to the police sketch, looking curious but unconvinced. *In for a penny, in for a pound.*

"He works as a security guard and he was at the museum on the day the Rosen painting was torched," she said. "He had a bad experience at the barn that was set on fire, and he's resented Marigold Grimm for the last ten years because he perceives that she chose me over him."

Cyn tried not to elaborate too much on that last point. She didn't want to drag Mari into this, and she should be allowed to come out to the community when she was ready - hopefully with Cyn on her arm.

Holt sat back in his chair. She was losing him. He folded his arms over his chest and said, "I know you're fire, not police, but there's such a thing as circumstantial evidence-"

"I went to his apartment last week," Cyn hurried onward. "There was a distinct smell of gasoline with no explanation for the source, and he had cigarettes that matched the brand we found in the Grimm House garden."

Holt shook his head. "You really haven't given me anything concrete, and arsonists are notoriously difficult to nail down. Did he confess to anything?"

"No," Cyn admitted.

"And do you two happen to have a beef with each other?"

Now, she did look away. "Yes. We've always had a fair amount of tension in our relationship. Our parents got married while my father and I were still grieving the loss of my mother, and I don't think Drew ever got a chance to properly mourn his own father's death."

"I'll look into it, but I have to be honest with you," Holt said. "The feud doesn't help, and I'm not sure I'm going to be able to do much with this information."

Cyn felt herself deflating like a balloon. That was absolutely not the result she'd expected. "Search his apartment. He's not that smart – I'm willing to bet you'll find something that will link him to the crimes."

Holt shook his head again, looking apologetic. "I can't

get a warrant without probable cause. Do you know why he's setting the fires? Our best bet at this point is to anticipate his moves and catch him in the act."

"Another fire?" Cyn asked, her heart sinking.

"Better one more fire than five," Holt said.

"He's upset about how his life's turning out, I guess," Cyn said with a shrug. All of the fires so far had something to do with her – the ways Drew believed she'd messed up his trajectory – but that didn't help her to predict the future. "He's mad at me because he thinks I'm stealing what belongs to him. Maybe he'll target me, or Grimm House again? If you can't arrest him now, then can you please put some protection on Marigold Grimm?"

"Trust me, Robinson," Holt said. "I'll do everything I can. I don't want any more fires, either."

Cyn nodded, satisfied. She stood up to go, then turned back to Detective Holt. "I know this is going to sound bad, but I may have gone a little vigilante."

He gave her a stern look – it reminded her exactly of the way that Frank looked at her when she got a little too eager at the scene of a fire and started thinking she was Wonder Woman, running in to put it out all on her own.

"What did you do?"

"I thought I could get him to stop if I gave him a shot at something he wants," she said. "I worked with Gus to pull some strings and get Drew an interview for a dispatcher position here. He's supposed to come in tomorrow – maybe you could sit in on the interview and get a little information out of him?"

"I doubt he's going to confess anything in the middle of a job interview," Holt said, but he didn't dismiss the idea out of hand. "I'll ask the chief if he minds having a second interviewer in the room. That all?"

"Yeah, that's all," Cyn said.

She left Holt's office feeling let down. She hadn't actually accomplished anything, and she didn't want to call Marigold just to tell her that she would shortly have a security detail. Luckily, there was Gus to distract her. He popped up from his desk as she walked through the bullpen, a huge grin on his face.

"What?" Cyn asked.

"What were you talking to Holt about?" he asked, looking entirely too pleased about it.

She didn't have the heart to tell him the truth – not right now, where the whole precinct would be able to hear it. "I'll tell you later, okay?"

Gus winked and Cyn gave him a side-long look. She wanted to ask him if there was something wrong with his eye, but then he said, "I think I know."

"You look pretty happy about it," she snapped.

Gus frowned. "Aren't you?"

"No," Cyn said. She leaned in close and whispered so no one else could hear, "Why would I be happy about turning in my own stepbrother? Or trying to, since Holt didn't seem to think he could act on it."

"Turning Drew in?" Gus asked. He had no idea what she was talking about, but the cat was out of the bag.

"Come here," she said, pulling him into the empty break room and shutting the door behind them. "It's bad enough I had to rat him out – I don't want the whole police department to know."

"Know *what?*" Gus asked, getting just as exasperated as Cyn felt.

"Drew's the arsonist," she whispered, and Gus's eyes went wide.

"Seriously?" he asked. "I knew the guy was a weirdo, but I would never have guessed that. Wait, that phone call about the job – was he blackmailing you or something?"

"No," Cyn said. "It was sort of the other way around. I thought if I got him a job at the station, I could force him to stop. Who in their right mind would keep lighting fires while they worked for the police? But then I told Marigold and she convinced me that I had to tell Holt before anyone got hurt."

She let out a long breath. *There. Everything's out in the open and there are no more secrets.* So why did she still feel so crummy?

"So, this is why you asked me to pull the work logs for Drew's security company," Gus said. "And Holt's not going to do anything? Why?"

"He said it was all circumstantial," Cyn said. "He's going to keep an eye on Drew and just wait until somebody catches him in the act."

"Wow," Gus said, running his hands through his sandy blond hair as if his mind had been blown. *Couldn't possibly be worse than how I feel,* Cyn thought. Then he asked, "Does Samantha know?"

"God, no," Cyn said. "And she'd kill me if she knew I

was here. You have to keep this information under wraps until Holt can make a move, okay?"

"Okay," Gus said. "*Wow*."

"Yeah," Cyn said. She reached for the door, then paused with her hand on the knob. She turned back to Gus and said, "Wait a minute. What did you think you knew?"

"Huh?" he asked, looking shiftily at the ground.

"At the beginning of our conversation," Cyn said. "You thought we were talking about something else. What was it?"

"Oh, I'm sure it was nothing," Gus said. "I already forgot."

"Bullshit," Cyn said. "Tell me."

They'd been friends since the seventh grade, when Cyn was a loner and Gus was a slightly porky, awkward kid. He'd never been able to keep secrets from her and she blocked the break room door with her body. It didn't take long before he tossed up his hands.

"Okay, fine," he said. "I'll tell you, but you're ruining your own surprise."

"What surprise?" Cyn asked.

"The service award winners are always announced on the night of the event, but I may have gotten some inside information," he said. "They picked you for Firefighter of the Year. I was flirting with Marcy at the front desk while she was stuffing the envelopes and I saw your name. I must have had a brain fart because when I saw you going into Holt's office, I thought he was letting you know that you won."

"Gus, you *are* a brain fart," Cyn said with a laugh.

"Just try to act surprised when they call your name," he said.

She was grinning like a mad woman, wondering how the hell this had happened, and then her momentary elation fell away and she said, "Shit. How am I supposed to accept that award while my own stepbrother is running around lighting fires all over Grimm Falls?"

TWENTY-SIX

MARIGOLD

On the night of the service awards, Marigold handed the final preparations over to Emily and instead focused her attention on Cyn. It felt strange, being in her living quarters instead of down in the fray as the first guests were beginning to arrive, but Emily would be officially promoted to co-conservator in a month when Mari's father retired and she had to loosen her grip on the estate sometime.

Tonight seemed like as good a night as any because Cyn was worked up about her award.

"I don't deserve this," she said as Marigold led her into the bedroom to get dressed. She was wearing a pair of jeans and a t-shirt, her dress uniform hanging in a garment bag over her shoulder. "I've only been in the department four years, and I don't think I did anything good enough to earn an award."

Mari positioned Cyn in front of a full-length mirror, then took the garment bag and hung it from a hook on the wall. She took Cyn's head in her hands and looked into her steely eyes, then said, "Just breathe. You *do* deserve this – you're incredible."

"Then why do I feel like such an imposter?" Cyn asked.

"Because your stepmom and brother have been treating you like garbage for years," Marigold said. "And that has more to do with their own insecurities than it has to do with you. Everyone else loves you... including me."

Cyn's expression softened and her lip twitched into a smile. "You do?"

"Yes," Marigold said. "It's crazy, I know, because it's been happening so fast-"

"Fast?" Cyn asked. "I've been in love with you since I was twelve."

Mari laughed, then let out a delighted giggle as Cyn dipped her over her arm and kissed her. When she returned Marigold to her feet, Cyn's arms were still wrapped tightly around her waist and Mari could feel the desire building between them.

She broke away after a few indulgent kisses and looked at the clock on her nightstand. "We have to get you ready for the ceremony."

"Just one more minute," Cyn said, refusing to let go as she kissed Marigold again.

When they finally emerged from the kiss, Mari watched Cyn change into her dress uniform, then straightened her collar and adjusted her tie. Then it was her turn at the mirror and she retrieved a shimmering black evening gown from her closet. She turned around to ask Cyn to fasten the zipper and felt her hands taking a leisurely detour over her hips, her breath hot on Marigold's shoulder. Then she finished the task and murmured in Marigold's ear, "Do we really have to go to the ceremony?"

Mari laughed and said, "Well, I'm the host and you're being honored, so I think we do."

"That's too bad," Cyn said, nibbling on the soft skin at the curve of Marigold's neck. Then she said, "I have something for you."

Mari smiled, reaching behind her to slide her hand between Cyn's thighs, but Cyn pulled away with a groan and went over to her garment bag on the wall.

"I hope you don't mind that it's second-hand," Cyn said as she pulled a jewelry box out of the bottom of the bag and came back to Marigold. "My stepmother gave it to me but I thought you would wear it so much better."

She opened the box and presented it to Mari. Inside, there was a string of delicate turquoise beads on a gold chain.

"It's beautiful," Mari said. "You want me to wear it tonight?"

"Only if you want to," Cyn said, but Marigold was already turning around so that Cyn could clasp it around her neck. As the cool beads slid over Mari's collarbones, Cyn looked over her shoulder to admire the necklace in the mirror. "I was right – they look much better on you than they ever did on me."

❄

THE BALLROOM WAS CROWDED when Mari and Cyn came downstairs. People were standing around, chatting and waiting for the ceremony to begin, and the chairs were filling up quickly with the service men and women that protected the city.

Some of them were still on duty. Two uniformed police officers stood at the doors to the ballroom and there were three or four more walking the perimeter outside the estate. Cyn had insisted on it – after Drew failed to show up for his job interview, she was convinced that he had more fires planned. Several weeks had passed while Mari prepared for the service awards and Cyn worked with Detective Holt to find a way to prove her stepbrother's guilt, but it seemed like Drew wasn't so careless after all. There were no more fires, large or small, and all had been quiet in Grimm Falls.

"I can't shake the feeling that he's going to do something tonight," Cyn had said as she came down the grand staircase with Marigold on her arm, looking all over the foyer for anything suspicious or out of place.

"Nothing's going to happen," Mari had tried to reassure her. "We've got tons of security – I think you're just nervous about your award."

"I wish Gus had never told me it was coming," Cyn said. "I'd rather have been surprised."

Mari and Cyn walked into the ballroom and a few heads turned their way. Mari's father waved to her from the front of the room and she was looking forward to introducing him to Cyn once the awards were over and the dinner portion of the evening began. Marigold started to lead Cyn over to say a quick hello, but then Cyn tugged her in a different direction.

"There's my dad," she said. "He's sitting by himself – I don't think he knows anyone here."

"We'll go get him and seat him next to my dad," Mari said. "He can talk to anyone so I'm sure they'll be fast friends."

They went over to Cyn's father and she introduced him to Marigold. Then he gave Cyn a long hug and said, "I'm so proud of you, sweetheart, and I know how much Samantha was looking forward to this event, but I'm glad that it's me who gets to see you accept your award."

"Me too, Dad," Cyn said.

"Is Drew working security?" he asked, looking around at the mix of private security guards and policemen who were mingling in the room. "He said he was working tonight."

"Here?" Cyn asked with a frown. She hadn't told anyone except for Marigold, Detective Holt and Gus about Drew's secret, but he wouldn't have the guts to show up here in his capacity as a security guard... would he? Cyn looked agitated as she glanced around the room, trying to spot him, and then she said, "Will you excuse me for a minute?"

"Sure," Mari said. Then she turned to Cyn's father and said, "Elliot, my father and I are sitting in the front row because I have to be up and down to the podium throughout the ceremony. It's a much better view – would you like to join us?"

TWENTY-SEVEN
THE BIG ONE

Drew took one last look at his apartment.

He'd been laying low for the last week, keeping his head down and going to his shifts for the security company so he wouldn't arouse suspicion. He'd thought long and hard about Cyn's attempt to bury the hatchet – or so she claimed – and ultimately decided to skip the interview she'd set up for him. For all he knew, it was a trap that she was expecting him to be dumb enough to walk right into.

That was the worst-case scenario. The best case was that he'd get the job, then be just as miserable as a dispatcher as he was as a security guard. More likely, they'd just laugh him out of the police station and Cyn could add the incident to her list of all the times she'd successfully humiliated him.

Tonight, he was ready to make his final statement to Grimm Falls.

He had a backpack stuffed with everything he would

need for the evening. He'd loaded the rest of his things into the trunk of his car – only the important stuff, the things he couldn't live without. There wasn't a whole lot inside the apartment that he would miss. As he decided what to bring and what to leave, he realized that there wouldn't be much to miss about a city that had been rejecting him his whole life.

He did grab the singed boots out of the back of his closet. Even though he didn't plan to return here, he was smart enough to know it was better not to leave a trail of evidence behind. He put the boots on because there was no sense in ruining yet another pair of shoes, and because damn it, he liked them. Once he got out of Grimm Falls, their history would fall away and they'd just be boots again.

And, of course, he took the lighter. He picked it up from the table by the door and slipped it into the pocket of his hoodie. One more fire, and then the itchy sensation urging him to flick the wheel might finally go away. The more distance he put between himself and Grimm Falls – or himself and Cyn Robinson – the better he would feel.

He'd go to a new town, get a new name, leave all of this behind him.

John Wilson, *he thought.* That's a common enough name to blend into the landscape, and it sounds like the name of a nice guy. Somebody people want to hire, and date, and get a beer with. I could be John.

He'd miss his mother, but this didn't have to be the end of their relationship. For a little while, he'd have to disappear, but once everyone forgot about him, he could set up an email account for John Wilson and explain it all to her. If there was one person in this world who would keep his secret, it was his mother.

If Grimm Falls didn't want him, then he didn't want Grimm Falls, either. There was just one more thing he needed to do here.

Drew closed his apartment door, but he didn't bother locking it. The police would be here soon enough and once he'd made sure his message was heard loud and clear, Drew didn't really want to be more trouble to anyone. If someone came by and stole his junk in the meantime, it mattered very little to him.

He was wearing black from head to toe. His favorite work boots were comfortable, with good soles for running. He'd have to make a mad dash to his car after it was done, so that was important. He wore black work pants and a long-sleeved black shirt to gain the element of surprise. He couldn't very well let people see him coming.

He hid his car in some overgrown brush on the side of the road, and then he walked, for what felt like ages. His backpack was heavy and sloshing with liquid every step of the way, and the night was unseasonably warm.

He was sweating by the time he came up the alley that would open onto Main Street, catty-corner to the police station. He crouched against the building and checked the time.

It was half past eight and the service awards had begun. Cyn would be there, along with most of the fire department and the police force. While they were all busy getting dressed up and congratulating themselves, Drew would be doing the real work tonight.

He took off the backpack and set it on the ground, crouching just like he'd done in the empty swimming pool. It was dark in the alley, so he'd be mostly working from touch. That was fine, he'd had lots of practice. He put his hand inside the bag and his fingertips touched the cool glass of a bottle. There were three of them, protected from breakage and wrapped up in scraps of fabric that would become their wicks.

Drew's heart was beating fast as he closed his fist around one of the bottles.

He had a clear sightline to the police station from here. All was quiet and there wasn't a man in sight. Perfect. He unpacked all of his supplies. He'd have to prep it in the alley because he wouldn't have much time after the first Molotov went flying.

He lined the three glass bottles up, then produced a plastic bottle of alcohol. He took the lid off and doused the three strips of fabric.

Then he took the lids off the three glass bottles. They were the last of the summer shandies he'd had in his refrigerator, and he'd taken great joy in emptying the bottles, envisioning their final use all the while. As he removed their lids, the odor of gasoline hit him and he wrinkled his nose. He really did hate that smell. He'd be happy to put it behind him once and for all.

He stuffed the strips of fabric into the mouths of the bottles, then he tucked two of them into the crook of one arm, held the third in his hand, and pulled the lighter out of his pocket. He flicked the wheel once just to test it. A tiny orange flame erupted and he grinned as excitement rushed into his head.

This is it. Time to pay, Grimm Falls.

He walked boldly into the street and flicked the lighter, holding the flame to the cloth wick of the first Molotov cocktail.

TWENTY-EIGHT
CYN

"Don't move," Cyn barked.

She got out of Marigold's emerald green BMW and ran between Drew and the police station. Her heart was pounding harder than it had at the scene of any fire and it looked like she'd arrived just in time. Drew was standing in the light cast from a streetlamp and Cyn watched for any sign of his hand twitching or coming closer to the wick of the Molotov cocktail.

She had looked all over Grimm House for him and talked to several security guards who had no knowledge of Drew being scheduled for the event. She'd taken her seat, heart pounding and knowing that she was missing something, and the award ceremony had begun. Marigold was beautiful and glowing as always as she called the evening to order and brought the police chief up to the podium to make his opening remarks.

It wasn't until a deputy that Cyn recognized from Drew's class in the police academy was called up to the podium for his service that it finally clicked. She knew Drew would be going after the police station itself, not the awards ceremony, so she grabbed Gus for backup and borrowed Marigold's car, then flew downtown.

The whole way here, she'd been thinking that there was still a chance she could end all of this without sending her stepbrother to jail. Now that she stood in the middle of the street and saw him with a lighter in one hand and a Molotov in the other, she knew it was all over.

"Don't do this," she begged while Gus waited, crouched behind the BMW and ready to act. "There are security cameras mounted on the police station – if you throw that bottle, you're going to jail for a long time. If you put it down, maybe we can get you community service or something."

"Community service?" Drew scoffed. "Please. At this point, I have nothing left to lose. I know there's no coming back from this, and you've already taken everything else."

For a moment, Cyn couldn't catch her breath. She was standing between Drew and his target like a human shield, and it occurred to her that she didn't know what he was capable of. What were his limits? *What if he threw the bottle with her standing there?*

"I've never wanted to take anything from you–" Cyn said, holding her hands up defensively.

"But you have," Drew cut her off. "My own mother thinks I'm a loser because of you. Couldn't hack it in the academy, didn't get the girl, can't even get her attention with a freaking Molotov cocktail because she's so busy jetting off to New York every other week. Meanwhile, she was ready to give you everything on a silver platter and you didn't even want it."

"Silver platter?" Cyn asked. "What are you talking about? She never accepted me for who I was, and the fact that she's in New York on the night of my award should be proof of that."

Her award... she felt a momentary sadness at the fact that she was giving it up to be here right now, but this was more important than standing in front of a room full of people and being recognized for merely doing her job.

"It doesn't matter," Drew said, then he hissed in pain as the lighter wheel got too hot and he was forced to let the flame go out. He shook his burned thumb in the air, then said, "Everything worked out for you in the end, didn't it? Perfect job, perfect girlfriend, perfect life."

"I wouldn't call it perfect, but I worked hard for what I have," Cyn said. She inched a little closer to him. If she could just take the lighter out of his hands, this would be so much easier. "You could, too."

"Stay back!" he snapped when he noticed her approaching. "I'm not an idiot, okay? I know I screwed up in the academy, but it's not as easy as you make it sound – I can't just try harder and suddenly get everything I want. All I can do now is let everyone know how I feel about it."

He flicked the lighter again, grimacing through the pain, and Cyn shouted, "Drew, don't!"

But it was too late. He touched the flame to the tip of the rag and it caught fire immediately. The whole world slowed down as Cyn watched Drew's arm arch backward to throw the bottle.

Then Gus came running.

He tackled Drew from behind with a flame-retardant blanket, throwing him down to the pavement. Cyn heard glass breaking and there was a scream – she couldn't tell who it came from.

Then everything sped up again. Gus had Drew pinned beneath the blanket, putting his weight on him to keep him down, while a couple more police officers came running out of the building at the sound of the commotion. They hauled Drew up to his feet and when the blanket dropped, Cyn saw a long cut running down his cheek where the glass had cut him and the gasoline seared into the wound.

"Call a medic," Gus told one of the other cops as he slapped a pair of handcuffs on Drew.

They dragged him out of the street and sat him down on the steps of the police station, reeking of gasoline. When Cyn walked over to him, he refused to look at her. The cut was deep, and he'd been lucky – a few more millimeters and he might have lost his eye.

"I tried to tell you," Cyn said, but as she spoke the words, she found that the undercurrent of guilt that she'd lived with ever since she became part of Drew's family was gone. *I'm not my brother's keeper. He was going to throw that Molotov at me.* She turned to Gus instead and patted him on the back. "I think I know who I'm going to nominate for a service award next year."

"Speaking of," Gus said with a grin, "Frank radioed

over while you were talking to Drew. He wants you back at Grimm House – police escort."

"Is everything okay?" Cyn asked.

"Yeah," he said, "but people are getting impatient waiting for you to come back and receive your award."

Cyn couldn't help grinning. With her stepbrother bleeding and in handcuffs on the steps of the police station, she really shouldn't have much to smile about, but in that moment, she could have jumped for joy. They were waiting for her.

"Okay," she said. "I'm going."

"I'm going to hold you to that nomination, Cinders," Gus teased as she headed back toward Marigold's BMW.

❄

BY THE TIME Cyn got back to Grimm House, all the other awards had been given out and the ballroom had been converted into a dining hall. The chairs were rearranged around the large, round tables that Marigold had used during her father's retirement party, and Cyn found Mari sitting at one of them with both of their fathers, who were making fast friends with each other just as she'd predicted.

As soon as Marigold saw her, she got up and ran across the room to her. She threw her arms around Cyn's neck and showered her with kisses.

"I was so worried about you the whole time you were gone," she said. "How did it go?"

"Drew was arrested," Cyn said. "He's at the hospital

right now getting treatment for a nasty cut, but he'll be okay. I tried to talk him down but it didn't work, so Gus did a heroic flying tackle and brought him down."

"That's incredible," Mari said. "I've been keeping your dad company. He's getting along really well with my father – they've been talking business since we sat down."

Cyn smiled. "Good. Oh man, I don't want to tell my dad about Drew."

"So don't," Marigold said. "At least not yet."

She gave Cyn a wink, then went to the front of the room, where the podium had been left in its place. She turned on the microphone and said, "Excuse me, can I have everyone's attention? There's one more award yet to be given tonight. You may have noticed that the Firefighter of the Year award was skipped over. That's because our award recipient was so dedicated to her job that she had to leave the ceremony to go be a superhero for a little while. She's back now, and I think we need to give her a hearty round of applause for catching the arsonist that has been plaguing Grimm Falls over the last month. Please put your hands together for the incredible Cyn Robinson."

The entire room erupted in applause and for the first time since she found out she'd be getting the award, Cyn smiled about it in an unreserved way. The people in this room were her family and they loved her, and no matter what Samantha and Drew had to say, or what her subconscious feared in her nightmares.

When the applause died down, Marigold talked about how she met Cyn in the middle of her own personal tragedy, beaming proudly as she recounted how Cyn had worked to preserve what she could of the garden.

"I was blown away by her compassion, which only continued as she worked tirelessly to do whatever she could to find the arsonist and help me recover from the fire," Marigold said. Then she added with a slight wink, "Of course, I later found out that her interest wasn't entirely professional, but if it took an early morning fire for the universe to bring us together, I guess it was worth it."

People chuckled at that and Cyn looked self-consciously across the table at Marigold's father, but he was smiling along with everyone else. Cyn's father took her hand and squeezed it, whispering, "I'm happy for you, and I'm so proud of you. Your mother would be, too."

"So, when I met Cyn's best friend, Gus, at the police station and he told me that I could make a nomination for Firefighter of the Year, I didn't hesitate to recommend Cyn," Marigold went on. "She's a dedicated firefighter and an incredible woman, and I'm so proud to be standing here honoring her. Now I'm going to turn it over to fire chief Frank Estes, who I imagine has some things to say about Cyn that are less colored with personal bias."

Everyone chuckled again as Marigold turned over the microphone to Frank, then she came and sat down next to Cyn and wrapped her arms around her.

"Thank you," Cyn whispered, giving her a quick kiss

that half the room observed. She blushed, then turned her attention back to the podium.

Frank talked about Cyn's hard work – including little things she didn't even know he'd noticed, like the time she'd gotten bored and begun digitizing all the fire department's old files. He talked about her rapid rise in the ranks over the last four years, and her role in tracking down the arsonist.

Wait til he finds out who it was, she thought to herself, but then she pushed that self-doubting thought aside and allowed herself to enjoy the moment as Frank called her up to the podium to accept her award.

The room broke into another round of applause as Frank handed her a heavy glass trophy with her name etched below the words *Grimm Falls Firefighter of the Year*. She looked into the crowd and saw none of the things that her nightmares had been preparing her for – her father was beaming at her, the rest of the town was clapping happily, and most importantly of all, Marigold was looking at her with eyes full of admiration and that pretty turquoise necklace in its rightful place on her delicate neck.

This was all that mattered.

As Cyn returned to her seat, everyone went back to their meals and resumed their conversations. Cyn's dad congratulated her, then returned his attention to Marigold's father as they talked about his impending retirement. It was the perfect distraction and Cyn took Marigold's hand, pulling her out of her chair.

"Where are we going?" she asked.

"To our own private celebration," Cyn said. "Your hosting duties are complete, at least as far as the podium goes, right?"

"Yes," Mari said, a smile coming to her lips as she caught Cyn's drift.

"Then let's go find your co-conservator and tell her she's in charge for the rest of the evening," Cyn said, sliding her arm around Marigold's waist. "There's one more thing I want to do tonight."

She brought Marigold upstairs to her living quarters and set her award on the entryway table, then scooped Mari up in her arms and carried her to the bedroom. She lay her down on the bed, the shimmering black fabric of her dress pooling around her, and then flipped her onto her stomach so she could slide the zipper down slowly, kissing every inch of her back as she went.

EPILOGUE
ONE YEAR LATER

To the untrained eye, the garden looked as if nothing had ever happened to it by the following summer. Of course, Marigold could still see evidence of the fire if she looked closely – there was the subtle charring of the paving stones where she hadn't been able to scrub away the soot, and the new plants had been thriving but they weren't quite as full or large as the mature ones they'd replaced.

It was an ongoing project, one that Cyn had gotten into after that first introduction to gardening at the teen center in the early days of their relationship. Mari taught her how to clone plants and deadhead the flowers at the end of the season, and they'd spent many a spring evening tending to the garden.

It was looking really good again now, and just in time for the most important event of the year – or as far as Marigold was concerned, the most important event that Grimm House would ever have.

She was wearing jeans and a t-shirt, kneeling in front of a little sapling that she'd grown in the greenhouse and transplanted to the garden this morning, when Emily came up behind her.

"I can't believe you've got your hands in the dirt right now," she chastised. "I figured you'd be running around like a chicken with its head cut off, your trusty clipboard in hand."

Marigold stood and brushed the dirt from her hands, then grinned at her and said, "Well, that's what I have you for, right?"

"Yep," Em said, then waved her phone at Mari, "except I live in the twenty-first century and I keep my to-do lists in the cloud."

"How's it all going?" Mari asked.

"Nope," Emily said, cutting her off. "This is my event – you had your chance to weigh in on how you wanted it to go, and now you just have to leave it to me. No questions."

"Fair enough," Marigold said. "I do have one question, though."

Em let out a belabored sigh and asked, "What?"

Mari grabbed her gardening shears and went over to the bluebell that Cyn had given her the previous year at her father's retirement party. She snipped a couple stems from it, then tied them together with a blue satin ribbon that matched one she'd secured around the trunk of the sapling when she planted it. She handed the small bouquet to Emily, then pulled a sealed envelope out of her back pocket and asked, "Can you deliver this to the bride? I believe she's in my office getting dressed."

"As you should be," Emily said. "The ceremony starts in an hour – at this rate, you're going to be late to your own wedding."

Marigold laughed, then went obediently into the house to shower and get dressed. It was bad luck to see each other before the wedding, so she'd arranged for Cyn to dress in her office instead of their shared living quarters, but it was killing her to go all morning without seeing her. Mostly, she wished she could see Cyn's expression when she read the note.

To my gorgeous bride on our wedding day.

As you walk down the aisle, look for the small sapling with a blue ribbon around its trunk. It's a hazel tree grown from a cutting I took from the cemetery when we visited your mother last fall. I wanted all of our loved ones to be here today, and now she has a place in the garden, too.

I love you and I can't wait to start the rest of our lives together.

Mari

Emily popped her head into the bedroom as Marigold was pulling her dress out of its garment bag and she asked, "Did she read the note?"

"Yes," Em said. "She said you better watch out or you'll turn into a romantic after all."

CINDERS

❄

CYN WAITED with her father on the terrace, her heart in her throat and a smile on her face that she simply could not wipe away. The rest of the wedding guests were already in the garden, their chairs set up in a large, flat grassy space in front of the trellis where Cyn and Marigold would be married.

"Are you nervous?" her father asked when he noticed her fidgeting with her tie.

He straightened it for her and she kept her eyes fixed on the door to the estate as she said, "My body is. My pulse has never been faster and my legs feel like jelly. But in my heart, I just can't wait to see her."

"I felt the same way when I married your mother," her dad said. "Enjoy this day – it's going to go by so quickly."

As if to prove him right, Cyn caught a flash of white through the window and then the door opened. Marigold came outside in a large, lacy gown that made her look every bit the princess that Cyn knew she was. Emily was walking behind her, holding up the train, and Mari's father brought up the rear, keeping the door open for them.

Cyn's heart skipped a beat and she wanted to run over to Marigold and kiss her. Instead, her father held her back and said, "You have to marry her first."

While they walked to the garden entrance, Cyn told Marigold, "You've never looked more beautiful. I'm so happy."

"Did you get my note?" she asked.

"Yes," Cyn said. "Don't remind me of it or I'm going to cry."

In fact, she'd cried once as she read the note, and she felt the tears welling in the back of her throat again, but she was determined to at least make it to the vows before she allowed the waterworks to begin anew.

When they got to the path that would serve as their aisle, the wedding march began to play from the clearing and Marigold hung back with her father and Emily while Cyn and her father made their way to the trellis first. She noticed the little hazel tree with the blue ribbon tied around it and managed to choke back her tears, and then all their guests stood as she marched past. She saw Gus, James and his wife, and Samantha, who wore a tea dress, a cap-sleeved jacket and a diamond necklace that almost certainly cost more than Cyn's entire outfit.

Drew was absent – serving out his ten-year sentence at the county correctional facility – but he probably would have found something to complain about if he'd been at the wedding.

To Cyn, it was absolutely perfect. The garden was green, the sun was shining, all her favorite people were here, and Marigold was a vision in her wedding dress. They had a quartet playing live music and the Scarlet Begonias were playing the reception, and Cyn had arranged for a surprise for Marigold – a horse-drawn carriage to take them at the end of the night to the luxurious hotel and spa where they'd be pampered before their honeymoon officially began the next morning.

It was the perfect wedding, but if they'd gotten married in an empty field during a thunderstorm, alone and caked in mud, it still would have been perfect.

Cyn's father left her beneath the trellis with the pastor, then found his seat next to Samantha. There was a little pause for dramatic effect as everyone shifted their attention to the back of the aisle again, and Cyn was the only person who noticed a pure white bird flying across the clearing and landing in a nearby tree.

Well, she was the only one who noticed the bird itself.

"Oh my god!" Samantha shrieked.

"What's wrong?" Cyn's dad asked as Samantha shimmied out of her jacket as if it were on fire. "What?"

"A bird just *pooped* on me," she hissed, throwing the jacket to the ground in disgust. Cyn tried her best not to smile, and then the quartet's rendition of the wedding march rose to a crescendo as Marigold appeared at the end of the aisle.

Radiant.

Beautiful.

All mine, Cyn thought.

Samantha's predicament was entirely forgotten and Cyn only had eyes for her bride. She watched Marigold come toward her, the large gown bobbing with every step as if she were floating, and time seemed to slow down. Cyn tried to commit every detail to memory – the strand of Marigold's fair hair that was tucked behind her ears, the birdsong coming from the tree branch above them, and the look in Mari's eyes that said she couldn't wait to reach Cyn at the trellis.

Her father gave her away and found his seat, then Gus and Emily came to stand beside Cyn and Marigold as their bridal party. Cyn and Mari faced each other and joined hands.

As the pastor made his opening remarks and talked for a little while about love, Cyn had the sudden urge to pinch herself. Just a year ago, she thought that Marigold had no idea she existed, or worse, she knew but she wasn't interested. And ever since she'd gotten up the courage to go back to the Grimm House with a couple of coffees and two sandwiches, she'd been living a fairy tale.

Was it real? Did this happily ever after really belong to her?

"I love you so much," Cyn whispered to Marigold.

"I love you, too," she answered.

Then Cyn leaned in and stole a kiss. She couldn't help herself – Marigold's supple lips were calling to her.

"I didn't tell you to do that yet," the pastor chastised and their audience laughed.

"I'm sorry," Cyn said. "I've been waiting my whole life for that and I couldn't wait another second."

❄

Keep reading the Sapphic Fairy Tales with Seeing Red

SNEAK PEEK: SEEING RED
HUNTER

"Come on, guys," Hunter yelled toward the ceiling. She was doing three different things at once, trying to shove her feet into a pair of worn nursing shoes, stirring a pot of lentil sausage soup, and preparing her nephew's insulin shot, which she knew would be a battle to administer if he ever actually came downstairs.

She was also keeping an eye on the little clock above the back door.

It was thirty minutes to six and on a good night, it took her twenty minutes to walk to the nursing home where she worked. Hunter's sister, Piper, was supposed to be home at five to relieve her from babysitting duties, but shift changes in this house were always chaotic. They never had any time to spare.

"Guys!" Hunter shouted again. "Dinner time - I'm serious!"

The boys were no doubt absorbed in a game of Madden. Aaron was eleven years old and completely obsessed with football. Josh was seven and didn't care one way or the other about it, but he never passed up an opportunity to bask in his older brother's attention.

In a perfect world, they'd both be doing their homework before dinner instead of playing video games, but that game console was one of the few luxuries they had – never mind the fact that Hunter was certain her degenerate brother-in-law Jed had stolen it for them. The boys didn't know that and Hunter could never bring herself to be the hard-ass who took away their toys and made them do their homework instead.

Their mother could play that role when she got home.

Any minute now would be great, Hunter thought, glancing again at the clock as she stomped her foot to finish jamming her heel into her nursing shoe. She'd gotten them from a second-hand shop and they were ugly as hell but comfortable - that had to count for something.

Finally, the boys came downstairs in a racket of heavy steps and Hunter had to laugh – they sounded like a herd of cattle stampeding through the house, making more noise than she would have guessed two young boys were capable of. Aaron had his first growth spurt over the summer and he moved in a lanky, awkward way that showed he hadn't quite adjusted to his new height yet. Josh followed in his shadow as they came into the kitchen and went over to the old dining table in the corner, plopping into a pair of creaky wooden chairs.

"Mom isn't home yet?" Aaron asked.

"No," Hunter said, "and if she doesn't get here soon, you're going to get your first babysitting gig."

"Paid?" he asked, to which Hunter simply laughed.

"I don't need a babysitter," Josh objected. "I can look after myself."

"You want to give yourself this shot, then?" Hunter asked, nodding to the needle she had prepared. He kept his eyes off it – he still didn't like needles even after two years of them – but he came obediently over to Hunter. She gave the soup one more stir and then asked, "Pick your poison – arm, leg or belly?"

"Leg," Josh said.

Hunter hardly needed to ask - the shots made the muscle around the injection site sore and Josh's doctor had instructed Hunter and Piper to alternate sites, but Josh had settled quickly into a pattern. Non-dominant arm in the mornings before school, leg in the evenings to keep his arm in tip-top shape for Madden, a game of catch, or whatever else Aaron had in store for him, and stomach never. It was the most painful option and Hunter didn't blame him.

Josh put his foot up on the lowest rung of a kitchen stool and rolled his shorts up to his thigh, then Hunter cleaned the skin with an alcohol pad. She administered the injection and Josh surprised her by being tough. He hardly even winced – probably because Aaron was watching.

Hunter set the needle down and tousled Josh's sandy blond hair, then said as he rolled his pant leg back down, "Good job, buddy. I told you it would get easier with time."

He'd been diagnosed with Type 1 diabetes right after Jed had gone to prison for a half-assed counterfeiting scam. Hunter had been in nursing school at the time and she'd dropped out to move in here and help Piper with the boys as well as the bills. Hunter got the only job she was qualified for – working overnight shifts as a nurse's aide in a long-term care facility for dementia patients – and even though the pay wasn't great, it seemed like after two years, she and Piper were finally beginning to hit their stride.

That is, if they could ever get their work schedules coordinated.

The boys weren't quite old enough to be on their own yet, particularly with the complicating factor of Josh's medical needs, so that left Hunter and Piper passing like ships in the night most of the time. At least one of them was perpetually running late for a shift. Piper worked at a café that served overpriced coffee to college kids at the nearby university and the tips were decent but the hours were irregular – what they really needed was for at least one of them to land a day job with reasonable wages so there would be someone at home to watch the boys every evening.

But that was a pipe dream and instead, Hunter was stuck tapping her foot impatiently as she glanced at the clock again and then took the pot of soup off the stove. It was twenty minutes to six and she would definitely be late again tonight.

❄

THE BOYS WERE SLURPING DOWN the last of their soup when the back door finally opened and Piper walked in. Hunter was sitting at the table with Aaron and Josh and she crossed her arms over her chest as she frowned at her sister.

"It's five minutes to six, Pipes," she said. "I'm going to be *really* late."

"I'm sorry," Piper said. "I couldn't help it."

She sounded out of breath and as she took off her jacket and threw it over the back of a dining chair, Hunter noticed that her cheeks were splotchy red.

"What's wrong?" Hunter asked.

She really did need to leave. She was fortunate to work for someone who was understanding when it came to her home situation, balancing two kids and a somewhat erratic sister. But over the last two years, Hunter had leaned on her boss's good nature a lot and there would come a day when her kindness ran out. There were a lot of nurse's aides in the city and it wouldn't be hard to replace Hunter.

Piper and the boys had to come first, though. That was the whole reason Hunter was here, and that meant *not* leaving her sister panting and flushed while Hunter went to work.

"Nothing," Piper said. She tucked a tendril of her bleach-fried hair behind her ear, revealing sweat on her temples. "I had to go to the bank after my shift and I had a hard time getting there before they closed. I ran all the way from the bus stop back to the house so you could get to work."

"Is everything okay at the bank?" Hunter asked, glancing at the boys.

In her life, things were very rarely okay when it came to money, but she and Piper did their best not to talk about that stuff in front of Aaron and Josh – especially Josh, who was the worrying type. Aaron was a bit older, used to seeing the adults in his life struggle, and he took for granted the fact that they always figured things out. The bills always got paid and he always had a roof over his head – which was more than Piper and Hunter could say for their own childhoods. That's why it was all the more important that the boys should never need to worry about the state of their finances.

"It's just that scumbag in the mortgage department,"

Piper grumbled, trying to sound unfazed. "You know how he loves to make our lives difficult."

"Are you still going to be able to buy my football equipment?" Aaron asked.

Piper and Hunter had been scrimping and saving for months to get him the jersey, shoes and endless other pieces of equipment he would need to join the middle school team. Aaron had mowed a lot of yards this summer to contribute to the cause and his coach had allowed him to borrow some equipment during practices, but the team's first real game was fast approaching and he'd need his own stuff in order to play.

Hunter hated the idea of disappointing him – they'd all had to make so many sacrifices in the name of Josh's health and she was really looking forward to being able to do something nice for Aaron just this once.

"We'll figure it out," Piper promised. "We always do."

"Walk me to the door?" Hunter asked her. She gave Josh a kiss on the top of his head and then squeezed Aaron's shoulder. Then she passed through the living room to the front door, Piper following behind her. They stepped into the tiny foyer, which was mostly just a three-foot-square coat storage space, and Piper pulled the door shut. Then Hunter asked, "Are we short on the mortgage?"

"Yes," Piper admitted and Hunter felt the news sink heavily into her gut. She and her sister had never been more than a paycheck or two away from broke but it had been a while since they were in crisis mode. It was nice while it lasted, she thought. Then Piper added, "I asked for an extension but our favorite scumbag said he can't do it anymore – the bank won't give us any more time."

"What happened?" Hunter asked.

"I don't know," Piper said with a sigh. "The usual, I guess – emptying bed pans and making coffee are not lucrative careers. Insulin prices go up every time we fill a prescription. Football helmets cost way more money than hard plastic and Styrofoam glued together ought to."

"How much are we short?" Hunter asked. "I'll ask Brenda if there are any extra hours I can pick up. Maybe I can work a couple of day shifts while the boys are in school."

"How many hours a day are they going to let you work, Hunter?" Piper asked. "You already do twelve-hour shifts."

"I don't know," Hunter said, grabbing her jacket from the coat rack. It was a thick flannel one that had been a good find at the thrift store, a men's cut that was plenty warm to get her through the winter months since she walked most places in Grimm Falls. "We have to get Aaron his equipment, though – I refuse to let him miss the first game of the season."

Piper nodded and Hunter thought that since she was already late, she might as well stop by the café on her way to work and pick up something sweet and caffeinated for Brenda – as both a peace offering for her tardiness and a bribe to pick up more hours.

"Maybe..." Piper started to say, then trailed off.

"What, Pipes?"

"Maybe I can find a way to get some money on the

side," she said. "I was thinking it's time to visit Jed anyway."

"*No*," Hunter snarled. It had been almost six months since she last heard her sister utter that name and even though they were still legally married, Hunter had enjoyed the fantasy that Piper had finally - *finally* – broken the spell that he held over her. Hunter looked sternly at her big sister, staring pointedly into her eyes, and said, "Absolutely not. We'll find a *legitimate* way to fix this."

Read Seeing Red on Amazon now

Printed in Great Britain
by Amazon